DEADLY RODEO THREAT

SAMI A. ABRAMS

LOVE INSPIRED SUSPENSE
INSPIRATIONAL ROMANCE

Recycling programs for this product may not exist in your area.

ISBN-13: 978-1-335-95761-0

Deadly Rodeo Threat

For questions and comments about the quality of this book, please contact us at CustomerService@Harlequin.com.

Love Inspired
22 Adelaide St. West, 41st Floor
Toronto, Ontario M5H 4E3, Canada
www.LoveInspired.com

HarperCollins Publishers
Macken House, 39/40 Mayor Street Upper,
Dublin 1, D01 C9W8, Ireland
www.HarperCollins.com

Printed in Lithuania

"Man, he's not happy about something."

The dog barked again.

Logan's gaze met Izzie's. "He's probably upset he can't help."

"He seems to have great instincts. If he hadn't warned us about the natural gas, we might not have gotten out in time."

Her neck prickled. *Instincts. Shadow had sensed something.* They hadn't checked for Lisa's body under the truck. Her insides twisted. She lay on her belly and ran the light under the truck. No Lisa. Her entire being turned to jelly at the immense relief. The beam of her flashlight caught something red. She wormed her way under the vehicle and swept the undercarriage.

"What are you doing?" Logan's voice filtered down from the cab.

Her lungs seized. "Logan, don't move."

"Copy that. What's going on?"

"There might be a reason Shadow is acting weird."

"You found her?" The catch in Logan's voice was unmistakable.

"No. I found your other worst nightmare."

Logan released a long stream of air. "Explosives."

"Affirmative."

"And?"

"Counting down. Four minutes and forty-three seconds left."

Award-winning, bestselling author **Sami A. Abrams** grew up hating to read. It wasn't until her thirties that she found authors who captured her attention. Most evenings, you can find her engrossed in a romantic suspense novel. She lives in Northern California but will always be a Kansas girl at heart. She has a love of sports, family and travel. However, writing her next story in a cabin at Lake Tahoe tops her list.

Books by Sami A. Abrams

Love Inspired Suspense

Tracking the Missing

Stone Creek Ranch

Christmas Rodeo Killer
Deadly Rodeo Threat

Deputies of Anderson County

Buried Cold Case Secrets
Twin Murder Mix-Up
Detecting Secrets
Killer Christmas Evidence
Witness Escape

Visit the Author Profile page at LoveInspired.com.

My flesh and my heart faileth: but God is the strength of my heart, and my portion for ever.

—*Psalm* 73:26

This book is dedicated to my childhood 4-H friends.
We had some good times at the county fair.

ONE

Sheriff Isabelle "Izzie" Sinclair gripped the steering wheel of her personal midsize SUV and peered into the darkness. Her headlights the only source of light. The heavy clouds, warning of a possible late spring storm, hid the moon and blocked the stars. The tree-lined backcountry road that reminded her of boney fingers reaching out to grab her sent a shiver rolling down her back. Or maybe the disappearance of her best friend, Lisa Russell, had kicked her imagination up several notches. What if the body reported was Lisa's? What would she tell her friend's twin brother, Logan?

"Are you sure you don't want me to assign Phil? An animal digging up a fresh grave—just yuck." The voice of the sheriff's department administrative assistant, Cory Yager, jerked Izzie from her creepy thoughts.

"I've got it. Besides, I'm almost to the GPS location you gave me." She glanced at her phone in the holder on the dash. "You said Mr. Hensen called it in?"

"Well, it was anonymous, but I could tell it was Rex. Let me know if you need backup."

"For what? To scare off the animals?" Izzie hoped the only animals were of the four-legged variety and not two legged. Now where had that thought come from? "Thanks, Cory. I'll call as soon as I know what we are dealing with."

"Be careful, Sheriff."

"Will do." Izzie hung up and focused on the dirt road. She scanned the sides, watching for deer. A crumpled front end of her vehicle from colliding with Bambi's cousin wasn't on her to-do list.

Her cell phone buzzed. She glanced at the caller ID and answered. "Hey, bro. What's up?"

"You disappeared from the wedding reception soon after Cooper, Grace and Lexi left for their honeymoon slash family vacation to Hawaii." Daniel's tone held a tinge of worry. Not typical of her full-of-life brother.

Once her other brother, Cooper, had his new bride and their eight-year-old daughter tucked in his truck, Izzie had waved and blown him a kiss as he left the ranch where the wedding had taken place and headed to the airport with his little family. Cooper and his new wife, Grace, had worked through the hurts of their past. Something she envied but knew wouldn't happen for her. Between her father's betrayal and her ex's deception, her trust in men, at least romantically, had vanished.

"I got a call from Cory about a possible dead body."

"Something I should know about?" Besides being her brother, Daniel worked as a part-time deputy, along with bullfighting during rodeo season and helping on the family ranch.

"Not yet. Let me assess the scene and figure out what's going on."

"Do you think it's Lisa?" Daniel asked the question that had rolled through her mind since the anonymous Rex Hensen had placed a call to the sheriff's office.

"I have no idea. Some days I think I made up her vanishing. But after Hope Horizon's mission headquarters returned my call a couple of days after Lisa supposedly left town and said they didn't know anyone by the name of Lisa Russell, I know better than to think she went to Peru." Izzie had received a text message from Lisa the day after one of Marshall County's preseason rodeos about a last-minute opportunity to go on a mission trip.

Not once had her friend mentioned she'd put her name in to volunteer until that moment. Strike one. And telling her over text and not in person. Strike two. "I know she's in trouble, Daniel. There's no evidence except her abrupt departure and Hope Horizon not having a record of her that says otherwise. Not a single clue. Even her truck is gone. But I feel it deep down in my bones. Something happened the night of the rodeo."

"I believe you, sis. And if it matters, I agree with you."

"Thanks." Hearing his affirmation calmed her runaway thoughts. "Go enjoy hanging out with our friends and family."

"Promise to call if you need help." Her class-clown brother could be serious on occasion. And now was one of those times.

"I will."

"I'm counting on that." Daniel hung up.

A few minutes later, Izzie slowed and parked her SUV at an angle. Her headlights caught the edge of the woods. She leaned forward and squinted out the front windshield. A leg protruded from the trees. Could someone say Alfred Hitchcock-ish? Not a fan.

"Come on, Izzie. You've got this." Great. She was talking to herself.

She slid from her SUV, retrieved her flashlight and pushed the door shut with a soft snick. Her gaze traveled the edge of the road on both sides. Her heartbeat went from a trot to a gallop.

Her imagination had gotten the best of her. She rolled her eyes. "Knock it off, girl." A couple of deep breaths later, her pulse slowed. "Get to work."

She rounded her vehicle and leaped across the shallow ditch. The jeans, tank top and her ever-present cowboy boots, which she'd changed into before realizing she'd be called out, didn't relieve the Texas heat pressing down on her. Late spring had been unusually hot, and the storm brewing in the distance didn't help with the humidity. Sweat trickled between her shoulder blades—a byproduct of living in Texas.

The hair on the back of Izzie's neck prickled as she approached the body. The odor of decomposition hit the back of her throat. She battled the urge to gag. The decay mixed with loam coated her tongue. She blinked at the tears pooling in her eyes from the offending odor. Slowing her approach, she waited for her senses to adjust—at least a little.

A shadow flickered in her peripheral vision. She stood motionless, studying the darkness. Nothing moved. The minimal light from her headlights left her wondering if her eyes had deceived her. Izzie placed a hand on her right hip, where her duty holster normally sat, but she had none of her equipment. Her personal backup weapon remained locked in the gun compartment of the SUV. Get it, or leave it? Deciding the creepy setting had gotten the best of her, she stepped with caution through the grass to her target. She aimed the flashlight at the human leg and ran the beam up the body. The woman lay face up on the ground. Izzie grimaced. The animals hadn't been kind to the female's extremities. Brown hair flowed across the woman's face, hiding identifiable features. Izzie's breath caught. Lisa?

She swallowed hard and brushed the strands away. A gasp escaped. Nausea roiled in her stomach. The lab would have to rely on DNA for identification. Izzie blew out a slow stream of air. The tattered and torn dress wouldn't be of much use either. But… Izzie squinted and moved closer. The necklace. She recognized the piece of jewelry from her investigation into Lisa's disappearance.

If Izzie wasn't mistaken, the pendant of a silver cross and gold barrel racer belonged to Carrie Norton, one of two barrel racers who'd disappeared from the rodeo scene over the past year and a half. Izzie's shoulders sagged in relief that she hadn't found her friend. But guilt edged in. The poor woman on the ground deserved her sympathy.

"Carrie, I'm sorry I didn't figure out what happened to you sooner. At least your family will have closure. Maybe you can tell me where Lisa is." She scanned the body one more time then stood and slipped her cell phone from her pocket to call for the coroner and a deputy to work the scene.

Heavy footfalls came from her right. She spun toward the sound. A fist connected with her cheek. Her head whipped to the side, and her phone flew from her hand. Streaks of white light filled her vision, and the metallic taste of blood coated her tongue from where she'd bitten her lip. She staggered, catching herself from falling to the ground. A thick arm wrapped around her neck and lifted.

Izzie's airway closed with the increasing pressure. Feet dangling, she clawed at the man's arms. *Think, Izzie. Think.* She grabbed the arm encircling her throat and used it for leverage. She lifted her knee and shoved the heel of her cowboy boot into the guy's shin. Or as close as she could without seeing her target.

The man grunted and stumbled. His hold loosened. Not stopping her defensive attack, she brought her elbow straight back and connected with his chest. It wasn't the placement into his stomach she'd hoped for, but the hit had the same effect.

She ducked out of the man's grip, but her freedom didn't last long. He backhanded her across the face and hooked her waist. Before she had an opportunity to respond, he threw her to the ground and wrapped his hands around her throat. His dark eyes glared at her behind the ski mask, but he said nothing.

The fight and previous strangulation had sapped her strength. She thrashed against his hold, but her body had met its limit. A black tunnel compressed her vision.

How had she allowed the man to get a drop on her? Some sheriff she was.

She had to find a way to fight back.

The headlights of navy SEAL Logan Russell's truck pierced the darkness as he maneuvered down the county highway on the outskirts of his hometown of Rollins, Texas, where his twin sister, Lisa, still lived. He hadn't heard from her in months. Granted, part of that fault landed on him. His lengthy deployment followed by the hospital stay in Germany after the mission that had taken the life of his buddy Monty and left him injured hadn't lent itself to phone calls.

In the past, even when he couldn't communicate, Lisa left him voicemails or sent emails on a weekly basis. After returning from outside the wire in a foreign country or on training ops, he'd return to base and find his email inbox and phone overflowing with messages from her. But two months ago, she'd gone silent. His worry meter had pegged the top. A phone call to Lisa's best friend, Izzie Sinclair, had solidified his concern. As soon as the navy released him from the hospital and freed him from his navy responsibilities, he'd hightailed it to Rollins. Maybe he'd overreacted. Then again, maybe not.

Shadow rested his snout on Logan's shoulder from the back seat. He reached back and sank the fingers of his free hand into the dog's fur. The black Labrador retriever had become his lifeline since he'd chosen to retire from the navy due to medical reasons. His last deployment had ended his career. He'd recover physically. But mentally? Doubtful.

Moments before the bomb had detonated, he and his fellow navy SEAL had fled the building. But the structure had crumbled, and a wave of debris had pummeled them, killing his brother-in-arms. Logan hadn't escaped injury. He'd recovered from his concussion, and his shoulder and leg were on the mend, but the survivor's guilt mixed with PTSD had done a number on him.

Once back in the States, his commanding officer visited Logan and brought Shadow with him. He explained that the Lab was a trained psychiatric service dog, and his owner had recently passed away, then gave him Shadow's leash. Like handing him the keys to a car.

Logan's therapist had mentioned getting a service dog, but

he hadn't accepted that he needed one until Shadow leaned against his leg. The dog became his grounding rod from that moment forward. And he'd like to think he'd returned the favor to the furry friend next to him since the dog had lost his previous owner.

During his recovery, he'd called his sister multiple times and had sent a bunch of emails. When she never responded, Logan had done the unthinkable. He'd called the woman who'd stomped on his heart. He snorted. Try *pride.*

"Shadow, I'm worried about Lisa."

The dog tilted his head and gave a quick bark.

"I know. Izzie's on it." Another reason his stomach turned somersaults. Izzie had shattered his confidence during his senior year of high school. He'd hesitated for years but had finally stuffed down his concerns about dating his twin's best friend and asked Izzie out. She'd turned him down flat. No explanation. Just a no. His pride had taken a hit that day. Five months later, he left Rollins and joined the navy. He'd only spoken to her a few times since. Usually while on a video chat with Lisa.

"How am I going to face her?"

Shadow panted in his ear.

Out of desperation, he hit the quick dial for his sister's number. The phone rang once and went straight to voicemail. He punched End. "Where are you, Lisa?"

He rubbed his healing shoulder then called Izzie for an update. The phone rang and rang, then rolled to voicemail. He hung up and called his friend and Izzie's brother, Daniel.

"Hello."

"Hey, Daniel." It was good to hear his friend's voice.

"What's up, man?"

"Did Izzie tell you about Lisa?" Logan flipped on his turn signal and made a right turn onto the back road leading toward town.

"We've been investigating but haven't found much yet."

Logan clutched the dog tags that hung around his neck. A reminder of his SEAL team who had his back even in the darkest of days. "Do you know where I can find Izzie? I called, but she's not answering."

"Hmm. That's weird. I just talked to her a little bit ago. There was an anonymous tip about a possible body out on one of the country roads. Let me check the location app to see if she's still there. Izzie, Cooper, Payton and I share permission."

Logan's hand drifted to Shadow's head, which was currently on his shoulder. The touch of his canine companion calmed his runaway nerves.

"Got it. She's still there. Maybe she left her phone in the car." The man quieted for a moment. "But that's not likely. I'll send you the coordinates."

"Thanks, Daniel. I appreciate it." He glanced at his phone. According to the GPS, he wasn't far from her location. "I'll touch base later."

"Please do. It's unlike her not to answer or at least text saying she can't talk." The sudden seriousness in Daniel's voice tightened the knot in Logan's stomach.

"As soon as I know what's going on, you're on the top of my list to call." Logan's sixth sense kicked in, and he refused to ignore his gut. It had saved his life more times than he could count while on deployment. He pressed the accelerator. The truck lurched forward.

"Thanks. Let me know if you need anything."

"Will do." Logan hung up. A mile down the road, he took a left onto a dirt path.

A moment later, he spotted Izzie's SUV. He squinted, scanning the tree line. Two figures struggled with each other. "Izzie?" He pulled to a stop and threw his truck into Park. "Shadow, stay."

He flung the door open and sprinted toward the pair on the ground. "Izzie!"

The man jerked his attention to Logan. The guy scrambled away and disappeared into the woods.

Logan dropped to his knees. "Izzie, can you hear me?"

Her eyes fluttered open.

"Are you okay?"

Gasping to refill her lungs, she struggled to sit up and whispered, "I think so."

He placed a hand behind her back to steady her. "The guy ran off. Take it easy for a minute and catch your breath." Relieved, Logan grabbed his cell phone and pressed the flashlight app. "Let me take a look."

Izzie wavered then lifted her chin.

Light aimed at her neck, bile crept up his throat at the finger markings and bruising that had started to appear. "I'm calling 911."

"That's not necessary for me, but call in a search for the guy who escaped," she croaked.

He raised a brow. "I'm reporting both. You most definitely need medical." He placed the call then tucked his phone into his pocket. Shadow barked. Logan glanced toward his truck and found the dog with his snout pressed against the window with a snarl. Odd considering the dog's marshmallow tendencies. "Let's get you to my truck. I don't like Shadow's reaction."

"Who's Shadow?" Izzie accepted help to stand. When she wobbled, he wrapped an arm around her waist.

"He's a psychiatric service dog."

"You have a service dog?" she squeaked.

"Yes. Now, please give your voice a rest." Once convinced she wouldn't topple over, he led her to his truck, opened the passenger door and slid the Stetson he'd brought with him out of the way. "Up you go."

Shadow sniffed Izzie's hair then laid his snout on her shoulder over the back of the seat. His tongue flicked her cheek like a frog catching a fly.

"You crazy mutt." Logan smiled. "Izzie, I'd like you to meet Shadow."

She placed her hand on the dog's head. "Nice to meet you." The words came out on a whisper.

"Shadow, best manners."

The dog huffed.

"Such a drama king." Logan shook his head then scanned the area.

Izzie's gaze searched the trees. "You think he's still out there?"

"Not really, but I'm not taking any risks with your safety." If the attacker knew what was good for him, he'd stay far away from Izzie. And if the guy decided to be stupid? Logan had the skills and then some to defend his sister's best friend. But for some reason, he got the impression Izzie would balk at the thought of protection.

Sirens floated on the night air, increasing in intensity as help moved closer.

Izzie's hand feathered on her throat. It burned on the inside and out. The impression of her attacker's fingers around her neck plagued her. Her breathing came in short pants from injury and fear. But mostly from anger. The man had surprised her, but that wasn't an excuse for a seasoned officer, especially a sheriff, to allow him to subdue her. Training had prepared her better than that. She couldn't stop the words of her ex, Criminal Investigations Group Deputy Chief Will Adler, from looping in her head. *You don't have what it takes to be in law enforcement. You're too soft. And a relationship? You're cold, Izzie. An icebox.* She regretted all the time she'd spent proving herself to the egotistical, chauvinistic, self-centered—

"Hey. Where'd you go?" Logan gently tapped the side of her head.

She blinked. Logan's brown eyes stared at her. The whine

of sirens came in loud and clear. "Sorry. Just trying to figure out where that guy came from." Her gaze traveled along the tree line. Where had he gone? Was he lurking, or had Logan scared him off?

"Speaking of, want to tell me what happened?" Arms crossed, Logan leaned against the open door.

Did she want to? No. Doing so meant admitting her ineptness. The last thing she wanted was for the man she crushed on as a teen to see her as weak and incompetent. She sighed and whispered, "The sheriff's department received an anonymous tip about a body. I came out to investigate the claim." She gestured to the leg sticking out from the wooded area.

Logan glanced in the direction she pointed. "I see the call was legit."

"Exactly. It's not a pleasant sight. The animals got to her." She closed her eyes, shoved the gruesome scene to the back of her mind and mustered all the energy she could.

"Her?" Logan choked on the word.

Her eyes popped open. "No. It's not Lisa."

"How can you be sure?"

"The necklace I found matches another missing woman."

"But—"

"The face is somewhat intact. We'll need DNA confirmation to be one-hundred-percent positive, but I'd stake my reputation that it isn't her."

Logan drew a deep breath. "All right. I trust your opinion." Logan motioned toward the medics and sheriff's deputy hurrying toward them. "Let the paramedics check you over."

"I won't argue."

Logan's eyebrows rose to his hairline. "Really?"

Izzie might've laughed if her throat didn't hurt so badly. "Really."

"Yo, Sheriff." Noah, one of the Marshall County paramedics, sidled up beside her.

"Hey, Noah." She cringed at the croak that came out.

Harper, the other paramedic, placed her duffel on the ground. "What's going on?"

Logan jumped in. "Some guy attacked Sheriff Sinclair. When I arrived, the man had his hands around her neck, strangling her. She escaped his grip, but not before he did damage. I'm sure she has other scrapes and bruises as well."

Noah's gaze whipped to her, and he whistled between his teeth. "Well, okay then. We'll check out your neck. After that, we'll discuss your other injuries."

Since she had nothing further to add at the moment, she nodded.

"Let me take a look." Harper clicked on her pen light and examined Izzie's skin then palpated her neck. "You're going to have some nice colorful bruising. Noah, grab an instant ice pack."

Noah popped the chemicals inside and placed the icy compress against her neck.

She flinched at the cold.

"Sorry, Sheriff."

Between the cold and the soreness to the touch, she struggled to hold back the tears that sprang to her eyes. She blinked, successfully holding the waterworks at bay. "It's okay."

Noah's pained expression obliterated her efforts. One lone tear snuck down her cheek.

"I know it hurts but hold the packet on your skin. If we get the swelling down, it'll feel better."

She swallowed and grimaced. Certain that if she talked, sobs would break through. The emotions tumbling around in her head from her brush with death had to stop. As a female sheriff, she had to rise above the reaction. Do better—be better—than her male counterparts. Something Will had drummed into her. More like shamed into her.

The Rollins community had seen her soft, caring side that

she allowed to come forward when dealing with the public. But she'd never let her feelings come out to play. Will had cured her of those types of responses, or so she'd thought.

"Izzie?"

Logan's voice yanked her from the past. She lifted her gaze.

"Deputy Wagner asked you a question."

Wow, when had Vince joined them? "Sorry, I was lost in thought," she whispered.

"No problem, Sheriff." Vince tucked his thumbs into his utility belt. "You have a lot on your mind after the attack. I asked for a rundown of what happened."

She straightened and set her jaw. "Get out your notepad or phone. I'm only saying this once." The whispered tone punctuated her words. She shifted the ice pack to another sore spot on her neck.

Noah and Harper cleaned and bandaged the cuts and scrapes on her skin while Deputy Wagner retrieved his phone.

"I'm ready."

Izzie proceeded to fill her deputy in on what happened. When she finished, Logan added his information as well.

"What does your famous Sinclair gut say about the crime scene and your attacker?" Deputy Wagner asked.

Wasn't that the question of the day? "Going off my initial observation, it appears the animals dug the victim out of a fresh grave, given the appearance of her dress and skin. My guess is you'll find the original burial spot not far from where I found her body."

"Why do you suspect that?" Logan asked.

"From the damage to her body…the animals didn't wait." She shivered at the memory of the horrific scene.

"And your attacker?" her deputy nudged.

"I'm uncertain. If he buried the woman, why come back?"

"We all know Mr. Hensen called it in. Could it have been him?"

Izzie shook her head. "No. Rex didn't do this. The man is an eighty-seven-year-old recluse. He wouldn't have the strength to do this much harm." She gestured to her neck.

"Can you think of anything else? An identifying mark. Maybe a tattoo or something?"

She hated to admit that all her brain power now focused on the throbbing of her injuries.

"Deputy Wagner, I think it might be a good idea to allow Izzie to process what happened overnight. See if she remembers more significant pieces of information after the adrenaline fades." She appreciated Logan stepping in.

"I concur. I'll take a look around and gather physical and photographic evidence." Vince stared at the ground, refusing to meet her eyes.

"What is it, Vince?"

He lifted his gaze. "I'll need images of your injuries."

"Don't be apologetic. I might not like it, but I know the job. Do what you need to do." Izzie had a newfound respect for victims of crimes. The humiliation of being the sole focus of the first responders had her fighting the urge to shrink away from the attention.

The paramedics finished tending to her wounds and packed their medical bags.

Noah handed her another pack. "You might want to get ice on your face as well." Noah drilled her with a stare. "Are you sure we can't talk you into a trip to the hospital? Strangulation is nothing to mess with."

"I'll be fine." She held up her hand to halt his protest. "I'll go if it gets worse."

He raised an eyebrow.

She chuckled then winced. "I promise."

Harper tugged on Noah's sleeve. "Come on, leave the woman alone."

"Thanks, Harper."

The paramedic nodded. "Just remember. You promised."

"I will." With her confirmation, Noah and Harper strode to the medic unit.

Izzie's shoulders sagged. Now, to get through Deputy Wagner's collection of photographic evidence.

"Okay, Sheriff, just a few pictures." Vince lifted the camera.

She held out her cut and bruised hands. He snapped the picture. She flinched at the flash. Logan moved closer, and Shadow curved his head and nuzzled her cheek. Izzie appreciated the support from both man and canine but refused to verbalize it in front of her deputy.

Several minutes later, Wagner lowered the camera. "All done. I'll grab the portable spotlight from the back of my SUV then head over and start processing the scene." He hitched his thumb toward the body and where she'd struggled with her attacker.

"Thanks, Vince. Call for backup. There's no way I want you out here alone."

"Thank you, ma'am." Her deputy sauntered off to finish his job.

Logan leaned against the truck door. "Are you positive you don't need a doctor?"

She wanted a lot of things, but right now, her concentration was on the woman who'd lost her life and on Lisa, not her own needs. "I want a closer look at the woman."

He opened his mouth then closed it.

Smart man. Because, at the moment, she had little to no patience to be coddled. Izzie lowered her feet to the ground and found her balance. "Come on. You and I both are worried about Lisa's disappearance. I want answers, and I think that dead woman is part of the puzzle."

"I'd like to hear what you've discovered."

"Once Vince's backup arrives, I'll fill you in." She halted. "I want to grab something from my vehicle." She itched to retrieve the handgun in her locked console. The vulnerability from earlier gnawed at her. She had to step up her game.

"Need help?"

"Nah, it'll only take me a second." Izzie secured her weapon and holster in the small of her back.

"Ready?"

"Yup." She slogged across the ditch and through the grass. Her adrenaline had faded, and each step weighed her down like walking in quicksand.

"Sheriff."

She turned toward Deputy Wagner. "What's up, Vince?" Her voice had gone from a whisper to a gravelly tone.

"I found your cell phone." He held it up.

"Evidence?"

"I photographed it where I found it and fingerprinted it just in case the scumbag touched it. But since it appears to have flown out of your hands and doesn't link directly to the attack, I feel secure in releasing it to you."

"Thanks." The distance between her and her phone felt like a chasm.

"I've got it." Logan jogged over and retrieved it.

She noticed he had a slight limp and wondered about the cause. Shadow nudged her leg. She glanced down into the black eyes of the Lab. Her fingers moved of their own accord and brushed the dog's head. "So, you're a service dog, huh?"

A pink tongue dangled from Shadow's mouth—a stark contrast to his black fur.

Logan held out her phone, and she accepted it. He gestured toward the victim. "How about you finish up so you can rest a bit."

"Sounds like a great plan." Izzie scanned the dark roadway and the surrounding woods. Was her assailant still out there? And *why* had he come after her?

Logan pursed his lips to avoid saying something Izzie would take offense to. As his grandmother would say, if a strong wind came, it would blow her over. His gaze never left Izzie as he followed her to the poor woman whose life had ended too soon. He balked at looking, but as much as he trusted Izzie, he had to make his own determination that it wasn't his twin.

"She didn't deserve this." Izzie crouched, wobbled and caught her balance.

He started at the woman's feet and moved his gaze up the corpse to her face. He'd seen horrible atrocities as a SEAL, but the ravaged remains of the victim made his stomach churn. Izzie was correct though. To his knowledge, the necklace didn't match anything Lisa owned. She wore his dog tags during races and a necklace from their grandmother the rest of the time.

"No one deserves this." Shadow whimpered from the edge of the road. Logan had told him to stay since he didn't want to compromise any evidence. "It's okay, boy. We'll be back in a minute."

"Your dog is super sensitive, isn't he?"

"He's aware of my distress and probably yours." Logan hated admitting his shortcomings, but in the brief time since the mission that took his friend's life and sent him home with injuries, he'd learned PTSD wasn't a weakness. Now if he could internalize the concept. "Do you see anything new?"

She stood. "Not without better lighting. The single spotlight and this flashlight don't help much."

Gravel popped. A sheriff's department SUV pulled off the side of the road.

"Looks like Deputy Bennett's arrived. Let me have a word with Jackie then we can head into town." Izzie strode toward her deputy.

Logan assessed the surroundings. Nothing triggered his concern. He called Shadow to his side and strolled to his truck. He ran a hand over the dog's head. A motion he did without thought. "Not exactly what I imagined when I came back to Rollins."

Shadow pressed into the side of his leg, grounding him so his runaway thoughts wouldn't stampede through his brain.

Izzie and Jackie had an animated conversation. The deputy nodded, shook Izzie's hand and joined Deputy Wagner.

"I'm ready when you are." Izzie met him at his truck.

"Where to?"

"That depends on where you planned to stay while you're here."

"I figured I'd bunk at Lisa's. She keeps her guest room ready in hopes I'll come visit."

"She misses you."

"Same. But the navy tends to keep me busy most of the year." Logan rubbed his eyes. "Now I wish I would have made more of an effort to see her when I could."

Izzie placed a hand on his arm. "We'll find her. We have to."

He swallowed the emotion that threatened to escape.

"I know it's late, but I'd like you to take a look through Lisa's house before you move in. I've already searched it, but since you're her twin, I thought maybe you might see something I missed."

"I'm used to long days." Well, he had been. His injuries had stolen his energy, and he struggled to regain his strength. "I'll meet you at Lisa's."

"Sounds good." Izzie left him to put Shadow in the truck.

Logan helped his furry friend into the back of his extended cab and hopped into the driver's seat. He pulled a U-turn and followed Izzie's SUV down the dark dirt road.

The crime scene played like a movie reel in his head. The image of the young woman's damaged body spiked his heart rate. What if he didn't find Lisa in time and lost her forever on this side of Heaven?

TWO

Logan dug his sister's house key from his pocket and turned the lock. Regret washed over him. Why hadn't he spent more time with Lisa through the years? The navy owned him, but he could've used his leave to visit. Instead, Lisa had come to him when she had paid time off, which wasn't often. He planned to change that if— No. When they found her.

Shadow nudged his hand.

He patted the dog on the head and stepped inside.

"How long have you had Shadow?" Izzie followed him in and flipped on a light. She withdrew her 9mm Glock from behind her back and entered the living room like a seasoned law enforcement officer.

"A couple of weeks. His owner died, and my commanding officer refused to take no for an answer. I think Shadow and I both need each other." Wow. Had he just admitted that out loud?

Izzie held up a hand. Her shoulders drooped, and her hand shook. If he had to guess, the adrenaline fade had caused her exhausted appearance. "Let me clear the house."

"Did you see something I didn't?" he asked.

"No. But I'm a little jumpy right now and would rather be safe than sorry."

"I'll go with you." Logan had no intention of leaving her alone until her strong, fearless side returned.

"You're unarmed. Stay here." Not waiting for a response, she left him in the entry.

"Shadow, I get the feeling she forgot I'm an elite operator. But I'll give her this one." He flopped the Labrador's ears back and forth. "Ears up, dude. Let me know if you hear anything."

As if the dog understood English, the teddy bear had vanished, and an intense animal emerged. He'd discovered Shadow had great instincts. The time the canine had mouthed his wrist and dragged Logan into the kitchen came to mind. He'd gotten sidetracked and left a pot of soup cooking on the stove. The smell had alerted Shadow, and the dog had saved him from a huge mess and possible fire.

A few minutes later, Izzie returned, and Shadow relaxed. "No one's in the house, and the back door is locked."

"Good to know. Now, how about you sit before you collapse in a heap."

She shot a glare at him.

He bit back a laugh, not wanting to antagonize her further. He'd witnessed her ire growing up. No thank you. "Let's sit and talk for a bit. Give yourself a minute to recover. Then we'll search the house together." He'd prefer to jump in, but Izzie required a moment.

She stared at him for so long that he thought she'd disagree. "Fine."

"I'll go make coffee." He halted her argument. "For both of us." Shadow followed him into the kitchen and sat, watching him brew two cups of joe. "She's a little touchy, isn't she? Of course, I don't blame her. She scared the life out of me." Shadow nosed his elbow and tucked his head into his side. The dog really could tell when his pulse rate increased. "I hope she still likes the fancy creamer." He found his sister's stash of French vanilla creamer singles in the cabinet and poured several into Izzie's cup. "Let's go face the storm cloud known as Izzie."

Shadow barked.

"Maybe you can get her to relax."

The dog trotted to the living room, leaving him in the kitchen.

Logan grabbed both mugs and found Shadow snuggling beside Izzie on the couch. The furball really did understand human language. "Hope you still like your coffee sweet." He handed her the cup.

Hands wrapped around the drink, she brought it to her lips and took a sip. "You remembered."

He remembered everything about her. The way she licked the icing off a cupcake first. Her obsession with flavored ChapSticks. The way she gathered her hair on the side and twisted it when she was nervous. "I did."

Izzie sighed. "Thanks, this helps." Her fingers scratched Shadow's head. "I'm glad you have him."

"Me too." Shadow had kept him from spiraling. He'd never forget the thoughtfulness of his commander. Silence lingered, and he tamped down his instinct to interrogate her about his sister's investigation. They both needed to unwind. "Lisa has kept me up to date—mostly. I know you were a detective in Dallas for a while and then became sheriff for Marshall County, but how long have you done that job?"

"Three years. The county doesn't have an election like most. The city council appoints the position. They interviewed and hired me like any other job. So far, I've stayed in their good graces." A sad smile tugged at her lips. "I love my job, so I hope I don't mess it up and get fired."

Where had that come from? This wasn't the confident, no-nonsense woman he'd known as a teen. There was more to her story, but for now, he wouldn't pry. "Lisa says you're a favorite among the community. I don't think you have anything to worry about."

"Maybe." The faraway stare confirmed his suspicions.

The air conditioner kicked on, and cool air streamed from

the vents. He let the silence linger, allowing her time to pull her thoughts together.

"What about you? You told me over the phone you were injured and aren't in the navy anymore. What happened?" Izzie brought the mug to her lips and sipped the warm beverage.

"Technically, I'm still in. But I'm on terminal leave. I was days from signing my reenlistment papers for another four years when my injury happened. Our unit received intel about explosives in the area, and my commander tasked Monty, one of my buddy's, and me to search the buildings of a certain town." Logan pursed his lips. "Sorry, the location is classified."

"As is most of your career, I'm sure." The tightness in Izzie's features loosened.

"Long story short, we found an explosive device. I tried to disarm it but ran out of time. The countdown on the detonator didn't allow me time to complete the task. Monty and I double-timed it out of there, but not before the device exploded, crumbling the building and instantly killing my friend. The collapse gave me a concussion. It also messed up my shoulder and gave me a deep bruise on my hip. Somehow, I tunneled through the rubble and waited for help." Logan's mind pulled him to the faraway place where he'd lost his friend. Shadow's whine and the lick of his fingers yanked him from plummeting into a flashback. "My team recovered Monty's body while our medic patched me up. We got out of Dodge. When I recovered enough to make a conscious decision, I gave my notice and declined reenlistment. I had enough leave to cover the rest of my current commitment. So—" he spread his hands "—terminal leave."

"I'm sorry that happened to you." The sympathy in her tone made his heart ache. "I'm glad you're okay."

"Mostly." He sighed and rubbed his shoulder.

She narrowed her gaze at him.

The injury still bothered him, but the emotional damage trumped the physical.

"Thanks for the suggestion." She lifted her mug. "I'm a little more stable now. The conversation and coffee did wonders."

"Glad to hear it. Could you give me a quick rundown of what you've uncovered in your investigation before we take a look around the house?"

She shrugged. "Not much I'm afraid. Other than Lisa's text message that I found to be bogus, we have nothing. She just vanished. No one saw or heard anything. Since her truck is missing, we can't confirm she hasn't left of her own accord."

"You know she wouldn't do that." His sister wouldn't drop everything and leave town. She loved Rollins and the people in it.

Izzie took a sip of her beverage. "True. But my personal opinions are subjective."

"I can see your point. Go on."

"Once Hope Horizons contacted me a couple days after Lisa disappeared, confirming my suspicions, I widened the search for other missing women in the region. I discovered two that fit. Carrie Norton, whom I believe we found in the woods, and Natalie Malone. Both were barrel racers who disappeared after competing in rodeos. They date back to six months and eighteen months, respectively."

Logan considered what she'd said. "That's a wide gap."

"It is. That's why I think we've missed someone or a couple of someones." Izzie closed her eyes and inhaled. When she opened them, fatigue stared straight at him. "Now you know the basics. I'm fading fast. I suggest we look around and see if anything stands out to you before we call it a night."

"Sounds like a solid plan." He stood and gathered their cups. "I'll put these in the sink to wash later, and we'll get started."

Izzie kissed his dog on the head. "What do you think, Shadow? Can your daddy find something I missed?"

Logan peeked back at the pair before entering the kitchen.

Shadow ate up the attention Izzie lavished on him. He set the mugs down and turned when he heard Izzie's whispered voice.

"I feel bad for Logan. PTSD isn't fun, but you help him through it, don't you?" She scratched his dog under the chin. "And you're really good at your job, aren't you?"

The black Lab tilted his head one way then the other as if to say *duh*.

Logan pretended not to hear the conversation and returned to the living room. "How do you want to do this?"

She patted Shadow's back. "Why don't you start at the front door and work your way through the house. Similar to clearing a building but instead of looking for bad guys, look for anything that seems out of place or missing."

"I haven't been here often. Only once or twice. I'm not sure I'd recognize something odd."

"You know your sister and her habits. You two have a special bond. I searched her place the day after she disappeared." Izzie shook her head. "I came up empty."

"I'm not sure I'll do any better, but I guess it's worth a shot."

He moved through the house, searching for anything out of the ordinary. Thirty minutes later, after examining the living room, kitchen, guest bedroom and hallway bathroom, he had nothing.

"Only three rooms left. Lisa's office, bedroom and bathroom."

"I'm praying I find something. Anything." Logan snapped his fingers, and Shadow responded. The dog trotted from where he'd stationed himself on the couch and plastered himself against Logan's leg. "Let's continue to work our way to the back of the house and hit the office, then bedroom and connecting bath."

"I'll follow you." Izzie held out her hand, gesturing down the hallway.

Silence fell between them as he looked through his sister's things.

Izzie leaned against the doorway, arms crossed. "What are your plans now that you're no longer in the navy?" She held up her palm. "Once your terminal leave is over."

Logan flipped through the papers on Lisa's desk. "I'm not sure yet. I've been doing rehab on my shoulder and hip. I haven't gotten far into my future plans."

"Have you considered coming home to Rollins?"

"Thought about it." He shrugged and winced. "Not sure what I'll do for a job."

"Well, that's easy." Izzie pushed off the wall and ambled to the bookcase. She ran a finger down one of the book spines. "Go through the academy and come work for the sheriff's department, unless working for me doesn't appeal to you. The police department would jump at the opportunity to hire you as well."

"That's a thought after I heal. But I'm not sure I'd be good at it."

Her hand halted on the book she was touching. "What is that supposed to mean? You have military experience at the highest level. You're an explosive ordnance expert. How could you not be great at it?"

"Like I said, I'll think about it." He had no desire to be responsible for anyone else's life. *Been there done that, have the scars to prove it.*

"I've heard that tone before—the *I'll say whatever to get you to stop bugging me*." She studied him for a moment then her gaze drifted to the window. She stared into the darkness. She hurried over and lowered the blinds.

"You're safe. You know that, right?"

She spun to face Logan. "What do you mean?"

"Just that I won't let anyone hurt you." He hoped he hadn't lied to her. "You might be the law around here, but that doesn't mean you don't need backup. Why do you think navy SEALs—

Team guys—work in teams? Because of the bond, we're stronger together."

"You're right. I wouldn't send one of my deputies into a dangerous situation alone." She sighed. "Being the boss...it's hard for me to remember that."

He arched a brow, waiting for her to elaborate, but when she chose to stay quiet, he continued rummaging through the items in and on Lisa's desk.

A while later, with the office a dead end, he worked his way to the main bedroom. Shadow appointed himself official dog sniffer and worked the room's perimeter, then decided to take a nap by the door.

"He's standing guard. Well, sleeping guard." Izzie chuckled.

Logan nodded. "Shadow takes his role as protector seriously. He's trained as a psychiatric service dog, but he's a guardian at his core."

Izzie used her knuckles to massage her lower back. The aches and pains from the attack had to have intensified over the last hour. He wanted to send her home to sleep, but he knew she wouldn't leave until he finished his search.

Logan opened the top drawer of Lisa's dresser, looking for anything out of place or missing. "I'll admit, I'm at a loss here. So far, I haven't found anything to confirm she didn't leave of her own free will." Logan paused when his eyes landed on the jewelry box on her dresser. He opened it. "Izzie."

"What'd you find?"

"Not found, but what's missing."

She peered over his shoulder. "I don't see anything wrong."

"My dog tags are gone." He fingered through the contents to make sure he hadn't missed them.

"I don't understand the problem." The crease in her forehead deepened.

"I had an extra set made and gave them to her. Lisa only wears my dog tags when she races. She's obsessive about putting them back." He gave the container one last thorough look and closed the lid. "When did you say she went missing?"

"Soon after one of the Marshall County preseason rodeos two months ago."

"I'd say we just narrowed the timeline."

Izzie sucked in a breath. "She never made it home."

"That would be my take on it." He placed his hand on top of the jewelry box he'd given his sister after his first paycheck from the navy. *Where are you, Lisa?*

Shadow lurched from his napping spot. A deep growl rumbling from him. The dog bared his teeth and snarled.

Logan froze. He'd never seen Shadow respond like that.

Izzie jolted at Shadow's aggressiveness. The teddy bear of a dog had turned into a grizzly. A shiver zipped up her spine. What if someone was in the house? Her throat constricted. She could feel the man's hands around her neck. The dark eyes behind the mask staring at her. She shook off the memory. *Get a grip, girl. Act like the sheriff you are.*

"What set him off?"

Logan held his fist up in a stop signal.

She halted her questioning and stiffened. The man had gone into full SEAL mode.

"Shadow, leave it." The dog quieted at Logan's command but didn't move from his protective stance in the doorway.

"He's not happy about something," she whispered in Logan's ear. Izzie slid the Glock from her holster and held it against her leg.

"Do you smell that?" The tension in Logan's voice sent a shiver up Izzie's spine.

Lifting her chin, she inhaled. She tilted her head and sniffed again. A sharp, sickly sweet tang.

Her pulse spiked. "Natural gas." Shadow latched onto the hem of her shirt and yanked.

"We need to move. Now." Logan grabbed her hand and tugged her toward the door.

Izzie re-holstered her weapon since a gunshot could ignite the fumes. One shot, one spark, and they'd be nothing but debris raining over the neighborhood.

"Shadow, with me." Logan led their small party down the hall and paused.

The gas thickened as they went. Heavy, clawing at her throat and burning her lungs. She lifted the neckline of her shirt over her nose and mouth.

"It's coming from the kitchen." Logan scanned the space ahead.

Izzie's gaze darted to the office door. "The window in there."

"Hurry." Logan coughed, covering his mouth with his sleeve. "If someone flips a light switch or the air conditioner kicks on, we're toast."

"Literally," she muttered.

They ducked into the office. Logan flipped the lock and hefted the window open. It scraped and screeched in the track.

Izzie held her breath, waiting for the world to explode. When it didn't, she exhaled. Her heart hammered against her breastbone. "Can we get out of here, now?"

Logan held out his hand. She took it and sat on the windowsill. She hiked one leg over the side and then the other. She dropped to the ground and spun to help him.

Shadow scrambled up next. His claws scraped on the ledge before he launched from the house.

"Hurry. I can't call for help until we're away from the house or my cell phone might cause a spark and ignite the house."

Logan ducked through the opening and hopped down. His leg gave way, and he stumbled.

She wrapped her arm around his waist to steady him. "You good?"

He nodded. "Come on, let's go."

You didn't have to tell her twice. She wanted nothing more than to get away from the ticking time bomb of Lisa's home.

They sprinted to her SUV, parked the furthest from the house, and ducked behind it.

Logan slid to the ground and leaned his head against the vehicle. His breath came in rapid pants.

She had to contact the fire department, but Logan's actions worried her. Izzie hurried to call dispatch.

"What's up, Sheriff?"

"I have a gas leak on site. I need Fire and RPD." She rattled off Lisa's address. Since the house was within city limits, it was out of her jurisdiction.

The clicking of a keyboard filled the otherwise silent line. "Rollins Fire and Police are on the way. Are you okay?" Leave it to Regina, her dispatcher, to add personal concern.

"At the moment. I'll touch base later."

"I'll let the crew know." Regina hung up before Izzie could tell her no. Her entire department would come in sirens blaring if Regina told them.

With RFD and RPD on the way, Izzie turned her attention to Logan. He stared straight ahead as if in a trance. The man hadn't moved since they'd escaped the house of fumes. In fact, he was perilously close to hyperventilating.

The dog crawled onto his owner, laid his furry body on Logan's chest and rested his snout on Logan's shoulder.

She watched in amazement as Logan's breathing leveled out.

Shadow licked Logan's cheek.

Logan blinked. Then blinked again. His arms went around his dog, and he closed his eyes. "Sorry."

"For what?"

"Losing it."

Izzie decided not to argue with the man. She'd say her piece later once things settled down. "Shadow's good at his job."

A half smile graced Logan's face. "Most days I don't know what I'd do without him."

Seeming to sense his task was done, Shadow moved to Logan's side and curled on the ground beside his owner.

Sirens wailed in the distance.

"Do you get the feeling someone doesn't want us looking into Lisa's disappearance?" Logan asked.

"But why now? I've been investigating since she vanished."

"The body in the woods. Could he have heard you identify the woman?"

"Maybe." She tapped her lips, thinking. "I didn't have time to call. He attacked before that. But… I hate to admit it, but I was talking to the body."

"You what?" He stared at her like she'd dyed her hair neon pink.

She scrunched her nose. "I told Carrie that I was sorry for not figuring it out sooner. You know, saying my thoughts out loud."

"I guess that makes sense. But how did he know you'd found the woman's corpse? It's not like he'd just buried her."

"That's a great question. One my brain might be able to answer if it hadn't shut down due to exhaustion." Her energy had waned, and she had little left in the tank after the events of the night.

Fire trucks and police cruisers came to a stop outside Lisa's house.

"Once we deal with that—" she waved toward the flurry of activity "—we can head out to Stone Creek Ranch. You can stay there. We'll dig back into the case in the morning."

"I'd like to hear everything you have if that's okay with you."

"I'll admit, I've hit a wall. And we'll have to wait on the coroner's report on Carrie to determine if there's evidence that can aid in the investigation. I'm more than okay with another set of eyes." She owed it to Logan and to Lisa.

"Thank you. I'd suggest doing it tonight, but I don't want to miss anything because we're exhausted." Logan hadn't stopped petting Shadow the entire conversation. She guessed the flashback or anxiety attack, whichever it had been, hadn't worn off yet.

Izzie agreed. She'd reached her limit. "Let's go talk with RPD and get out of here." She stood and grimaced. Her body ached, and her face hurt. Resting rose on her priority list. To help Lisa, she had to be at the top of her game. And right now, she was anything but.

THREE

Logan's hands tightened around the steering wheel as he drove into town after spending the night at the ranch. Shadow lay in the back of the extended cab tethered to his harness with a doggie seat belt while Izzie occupied the passenger's seat. He'd woken later than usual but allowed Izzie to sleep while he made coffee and fed his dog. She required rest to heal, something he was well aware of. But the dark circles under her eyes worried him. She'd played it off as a few aches, but he knew she hurt. Why the woman wouldn't be honest with him about her pain level, he had no idea.

Last night, he and Izzie had agreed to go over the information she'd collected that related to Lisa's disappearance. But after mulling it over while he stared at the ceiling in the middle of the night, he'd requested a fresh look. So instead of heading to the sheriff's office, they planned to visit the rodeo grounds where Lisa had last been seen.

He glanced at Izzie for the twentieth time. "Are you sure you're up for this?"

She stiffened. "Why wouldn't I be?"

"Oh, I don't know. You have bruises everywhere, and I know for a fact your throat is sore. You grimace when you swallow." Man, she was prickly this morning. He hadn't remembered her having a touchy side. But years had passed. Life happened. People changed. He knew he had. The confidence he'd gained during his years as an active SEAL had evaporated with his failure on the last mission. He'd become more cautious and questioned his judgment more frequently since that day.

"I can do my job." Her tone held a bite that surprised him.

"I never said you couldn't." He sighed. "Look, Izzie, I'm not saying these things to start an argument. I'm concerned. That's all."

Her shoulders drooped. "Sorry. I'm...well... I'm not at the top of my game. And I hate feeling incompetent."

Yup, that statement screamed of a hidden meaning, but he'd let it go—for now. "How about we start the morning over?"

Izzie shifted to face him. "Explain."

"This." He flashed her a smile. "Izzie, I want to make sure you're doing okay. How are you feeling?"

She studied him a moment, then followed his lead. "I'm sore, but overall, fine."

"Good. I'm happy to hear that." He glanced at her, then back to the road. "See, was that so hard?"

Her lips pursed, and her shoulders shook.

Shadow's head popped over the seat at some point during their mini argument. The dog studied Izzie then looked at Logan as if to ask, *Is she okay?* The dog had proven to be quite expressive.

"You hold that laugh in much longer, and your ribs will ache even more."

A chuckle filled the cab. Shadow swiped a wet tongue up Izzie's cheek. Her laugh turned into a giggle. "Eww, Shadow." She wiped the slobber from her face and shifted to face Logan. "Thank you."

"For what?"

"Not treating me like a wilting flower."

He chuffed. "As if. You're Izzie. Champion barrel racer, ranch hand and the Marshall County sheriff. I don't see anything weak about you."

Her eyes widened. "That's how you see me?"

"Of course. Even as a teen, you had a strength I admired."

Her forehead scrunched. "I guess."

What in the world had happened to cause her to question herself? "I've been in and out of contact with Lisa due to deployments. We talked when possible, but I have to admit, I haven't been the brother I should have." When they found his sister alive—because the alternative was unacceptable—he planned to change that. "She spent a lot of time at the rodeos, right?"

Izzie nodded. "She barrel raced in some but worked with the younger girls as well, mentoring the next generation."

"That sounds like her." He tapped his thumb on the steering wheel. "Did she have a boyfriend?" Logan didn't think so, but he'd ask.

"Not really." Izzie watched the scenery go by as he drove to the rodeo grounds.

"What does that mean?"

"She's dated a few guys. But nothing serious."

"All cowboys?"

"Mostly. But a few guys came to the feedstore where she works. One was a sales rep. The other…" Izzie's mouth twisted. "I believe the guy came in for dog supplies like a collar or leash and toys. I can't remember. He didn't fit the standard cowboy or country persona. I have no idea what he does. Another was Raymond Burke, a graphic designer. According to him, he came to town to take care of his friend's father after his friend, Hudson, died in an accident. Raymond never left. His job allows him to work from anywhere as long as he has Wi-Fi."

"She dated all these dudes?" Horrible scenarios swirled in his mind. What had Lisa been thinking? She knew better than that.

Izzie raised an eyebrow. "If you call a cup of coffee at Saddle Sips a date, then yes."

"Sorry. That does sound like her and her outgoing self." A coffee shop with people coming in and out. Okay, so he'd jumped to conclusions. "So we should add the owner of the coffee shop to our interview list?"

"I've already talked to her. But if you'd like, after we hit the rodeo grounds, we'll head over and chat with Annie. She took over when her parents decided to sell the shop."

"Mr. and Mrs. Faust retired?"

She nodded. "Annie has taken it to a new level, modernizing the business."

"That has to be good for Rollins." He slowed as he maneuvered through downtown and headed toward the rodeo grounds.

"It is. A lot of the other stores on the square have followed her lead."

Several minutes later, Logan pulled into the parking lot and chose a space close to the barn. "I want to get a feel for the place and ask a few questions, but you're the law around here. How do you want to handle it?"

"Keep the conversations low-key. I've already questioned everyone two months ago. I don't want to stir up rumors. The last thing we need is more speculation." Izzie straightened in her seat, looking more at ease than a few minutes ago. Her choice of jeans and a Marshall County Sheriff's polo shirt this morning was not what he expected. Not a typical sheriff look, but it fit her personality.

Happy to see her morph into the self-assured woman he'd once known, he'd agreed without hesitation. Besides, he didn't plan to interrogate anyone. Just ask a few questions to get the feel of what happened. "That works."

He exited his truck and helped Shadow from the back. He grabbed his Stetson off the seat and placed it on his head. The navy might be in his blood and have taken him abroad, but he was a Texan through and through.

The dog trotted next to them on full duty, decked out in his service vest, as they strode into the barn where the cowboys and cowgirls kept their horses. The buzz of activity surprised

Logan. He hadn't expected the number of people working here this time of day.

"Shadow, with me." The dog panted, and his tail wagged, but he obeyed Logan's command.

The smell of hay and horse tickled his nose, bringing back memories of his teen years. He'd never competed at the level Lisa and Izzie had. He'd tried his hand at steer wrestling during high school rodeos for fun, but he'd known his talents didn't extend to the rodeo circuit.

Izzie approached a footlocker. "This is Lisa's. I've searched it but feel free." She unlocked it and stood to the side. "We took her horse Cricket to the ranch. Everyone out there cares for him. He's getting a bit spoiled. I take him out and run barrels with him once a week so that he doesn't get out of practice."

"Thank you for that. Cricket means the world to Lisa." Logan sifted through the contents of the box. Nothing out of the ordinary as far as he was concerned. Just her normal gear. "No dog tags."

"That means she had them with her."

"Going with the assumption that someone abducted her, that's evidence that whoever took her did it after her race and before she arrived at home." Logan closed and locked the container.

"Hey, Sheriff." A man with a black Stetson, nice jeans and a navy blue Western shirt strode their way.

"Heath. How's it going?"

"Good."

"I don't think you've met Logan Russell, Lisa's twin brother."

"Nice to meet you." Heath held out his hand, and Logan shook it.

"Likewise."

"I came to check on Comet before I head out to meet with a client, so I better get busy." Heath moved to his horse's stall.

"Business good?" Izzie asked.

"Very." Heath added a flake of alfalfa to his horse's stall, petted the animal, then dusted off his hands. "Better get moving or I'll be late. Just wanted to make sure Comet had plenty of water."

"See you later."

Heath waved and strode off.

Logan watched the man exit the barn. "I couldn't tell if he was overdressed or underdressed for work."

Izzie grinned. "He's a livestock agent. I'd say with that shirt, he's meeting a *new* client."

"If you say so."

"There's a couple of Lisa's protégés." Izzie pointed to two young women. "Let me introduce you."

He'd guess the pair were eighteen, maybe twenty years old, if that.

"Come on." Izzie veered toward the girls. Dust kicked up beneath her boots. "Hey, ladies."

"Hi, Sheriff Sinclair. Who's the cute dog?" The brunette greeted them while the redhead waved.

"This is Shadow." Logan patted the dog's head then gave him a hand signal, freeing him to greet the girls. Shadow bound over to them. "I'm Logan, Lisa Russell's brother."

The girls smiled and loved on the dog until Logan snapped his fingers. Shadow dutifully returned to his side.

"How's the barrel racing going, Courtney?" Izzie asked.

The brunette beamed. "It's great. We're doing so much better."

"I'm sure Lisa would be proud of you. And you too, Lena."

The redhead's gaze dropped to the ground. "Probably, but we haven't seen her in months."

"We're worried about her." Courtney's forehead creased. "We thought she'd be back by now."

"As are we." Logan wanted to shake the girl and ask what she knew. But his training kicked in, and he masked his emotions.

"I know we've talked, but Logan wanted to ask you a few questions." Izzie gave him an opening.

"Sure." Lena shrugged.

"Did either of you see Lisa the night she left?" Logan asked.

Courtney shook her head. "She stayed until the barrel racing finished, but I didn't see her after that."

"Doesn't she normally stay through all of the events?" Lisa loved rodeo life. Her leaving early struck him as odd.

"Most of the time, unless she has to open at the feedstore the next day," Lena said.

He tucked that information away to ask Izzie about later. "Was she dating anyone?"

Courtney glanced at Izzie then at him. "She went out with Isaac a couple of times, but they aren't a thing."

"Isaac Sample?" Izzie seemed a bit surprised—which confused *him*.

Logan stared at Izzie. "You know this guy?"

"Well, yeah, he rides broncs. He's competed on the circuit for years."

"What's your opinion of him?" His gaze drifted from one woman to the next.

Courtney held out her hands, palms up. "Isaac's a good guy. He likes to have fun but is always respectful."

"That sounds about right," Izzie agreed. "Anyone else?"

The entire conversation baffled Logan. He cocked his head. Izzie and Lisa were best friends. Wouldn't she know all this? Or at least have found out while investigating?

"Not really. She hung out in the barn a lot. She's outgoing. Everyone likes her." Lena put her thumbs in the front pockets of her jeans.

"She used to have a thing for bull riders. Is that still the case?" Logan remembered his sister's fascination with the men who dared to climb on the back of a two-thousand-pound animal. He never understood the desire to risk life and limb to ride bulls.

The younger women chuckled.

Izzie smiled. "In general, the riders are younger. A bit out of her age group and a little too full of themselves for her."

The women nodded.

"Got it." Logan ran a hand behind his neck. "Anything else you can think of?"

Lena's shoulders drooped. "Do you think she's okay?"

Izzie sighed. "To be honest, Lena, I don't know. But I'm doing everything I can to find her."

"Sorry we couldn't help." Courtney shoved her hands into her back pockets.

"I appreciate you talking with me. It helped me more than you know to hear about my sister." Logan shifted to face Izzie. "Shall we go?"

Izzie nodded. "Thanks, ladies." She waved at the girls and strode away, gesturing for him to follow.

Logan joined her with Shadow trotting along at his side.

Izzie leaned in. "That's the first I've heard about her and Isaac dating. No one mentioned it two months ago."

"Did she keep it a secret from you?"

She shook her head. "I don't know. But remember, I'm not around the rodeo as much as I used to be now that I'm the sheriff. Could be they weren't really dating but just hanging out after the rodeos."

"Maybe." He'd let that idea marinate for a bit.

Izzie's shoulders drooped as they strode from the barn. "Let's head to Saddle Sips. I'll reintroduce you to Annie, and you can ask a few questions if you'd like."

The increased fatigue in Izzie's features hadn't escaped him. But he'd keep that comment to himself. He'd stepped in that minefield earlier and refused to give her a reason to give him another cold shoulder. He still had no idea what he'd done as a teen to have her reject him.

"Then let's go. I could use a cup of coffee." He snapped his fingers, and Shadow attached himself to Logan's left side as he steered Izzie toward his truck. He glanced at his watch. An hour of wasted time, and they were no closer to figuring out what happened to his twin. Deep down in his gut, he knew time was running out.

The street buzzed with people going to and from work, along with those shopping at the downtown stores of Rollins. Izzie slid from Logan's truck. Under normal circumstances, she enjoyed visiting Main Street. She placed her fists into her lower back and arched. A ripple of snaps sounded like someone popping plastic bubble wrap. The relief to her lower back was immediate, but the stretch had ignited an intense burn in her injuries. The visible bruises on her body worried her. What would people say? But covering them would be impossible. Not much she could do about the small V in her work polo collar exposing the black-and-blue finger marks where the attacker had strangled her. Her heart rate kicked up a notch at the thought of the man who almost killed her. Was he someone she knew? A member of the community? She scanned the area with a practiced law enforcement eye.

Logan skirted the front of the truck with Shadow by his side. "Doing okay?"

"I'm fine." She closed her eyes and sighed. She'd let fear take hold and hadn't meant to bark at him. "Sorry. That was rude."

"Give yourself a break. You're allowed to be on edge after what happened." He scratched between Shadow's ears, and she was certain the dog's eyes rolled back in his head at the attention his owner gave him. "Come on. I don't know about you, but I could use a good cup of joe."

Thankful that Logan hadn't taken her snippiness personally, she joined him on the curb, and they strode the short distance down the sidewalk to the coffee shop.

A bell jingled above, and Logan held the door open. Izzie

loved the old-fashioned bell. It gave the place character. On the other hand, the inside had a modern vibe, with a few features of years gone by mixed in. The combination of old and new worked. Annie had done a fabulous job decorating the place.

Izzie entered and smiled at the hustle and bustle. "Annie's an amazing businesswoman. She took over and created a place where the townspeople can enjoy time together."

"I'm a bit shocked at the busyness. When did Rollins step into this century?" He placed his hand on the small of her back and led her to the end of the line to order.

She chuckled. "A few younger owners took over the shops in town and have brought life back into the community." Izzie gestured to a table with six older women. "Those ladies over there are from church. They meet every Monday, Wednesday and Friday like clockwork. Sometimes for friendly gossip, other times to plan an upcoming event."

"And those guys?" He jutted his chin toward a small group of men.

"Those are the rodeo board members. You know Donovan Keats, the director. He's been here forever. The others change from year to year. But, at the moment, you have Wilson Henry in the red shirt, Lyle Krane has the black hair and the younger man is Trevor Osborne." She glanced around the room. "Grey Chapman is usually here, but he appears to be missing today. You met Heath O'Brien this morning. He and Richard Monohan are deep in conversation by the window. Most likely deciding what animals to purchase next. O'Brien's a livestock agent and Monohan manages a small farm on the edge of Marshall County. Oh, and the man sitting by himself in the corner is Harvey Powers. He's a loner. Lost his wife and child in a car accident a few years ago. He's never quite been the same. I'm happy to see him out and about."

They shuffled forward on the line to order. "Do you know what you want?" he asked.

"Of course. This is my second home most days."

His eyebrow arched. "I didn't take you for a coffee snob."

She slapped a hand over her heart. "I'm wounded. Just because I have a discerning palate doesn't make me a snob. I'm a connoisseur."

"If you say so." He smiled. "So, what's good?"

"Everything. But my favorite is an iced dark brew with sweet cream. And if I'm really adventurous, I add the pastry of the day. You can't go wrong with anything Annie makes."

"Sounds good."

When they reached the counter, Izzie placed their order, including the day's special treat, and requested a conversation with Annie when she was available. The barista promised to pass along the message.

Once seated in the corner with a view of the entire room and Shadow tucked under the table, she took a sip of her go-to warm-weather drink and scanned the shop.

"This place really is hopping." His eyes roamed the room as he sipped his drink. "Mmm, this is good. Sure does beat navy swill."

"I told you." Izzie took a bite of the blackberry cream cheese Danish and melted into her seat. The sugary goodness comforted her. She and Logan sat in silence as they ate. Her mind chose that time to spin about her near-death experience last night and the implication of the missing dog tags. How had the attacker known she'd investigate the body? Or had it been a coincidence that he was checking on or visiting his victim? If so, the man had to be living or staying nearby. Izzie stiffened. The person responsible for her scrapes and bruises could be anyone in town. How else would they have arrived at the crime scene so quickly? She examined each person in the shop.

"What brought on that reaction?"

She flipped her attention to Logan. "What are you talking about?"

"The panic that flitted across your face." Logan's gaze drifted from person to person. "You think the person that tried to kill you last night is here?"

She patted the air. "Shh. Not so loud. I don't want the town to know what happened to me."

Logan chuckled.

She glared at him. "Stop laughing at me."

"I'm not laughing *at* you. I'm amused by the thought that anything in a small town can be kept under wraps."

Her shoulders sagged. "You have a point. I don't want people to think I'm not able to do my job as sheriff."

"Why would they? From what I've heard and witnessed so far, you're good. Really good."

"Thanks. But I still don't want to tarnish my reputation by showing my inability to defend myself."

"You're really worried about that, aren't you?"

"Of course I am. This county might not elect their sheriff, but the town council who hired me can fire me if they feel I'm not up to the job. I never want my competence in doubt."

Logan studied her like he had super X-ray vision and could see straight through her. She squirmed in her seat, not liking the intensity of his gaze.

Annie approached, saving her from spilling her secrets. "Hi, Sheriff."

"Hey, Annie. Thanks for coming to join us." Izzie gestured to the empty chair. "This is Logan Russell, Lisa's twin brother."

"I remember Logan from high school. It's good to see you again." Annie shook his hand and sat at the table. "Lisa's a sweetheart. So, what can I do for the two of you?"

"As you know, I believe Lisa is missing." Izzie placed her cup on the table. "I've been investigating what happened to her for the past two months. But I want to review everything we have so far. And since Logan is here, I want his input. Please tell him what you told me about the last time you saw her."

"Let me think." The creases in Annie's forehead deepened. "She had a coffee date with Grey a couple days before she disappeared. Around that same time, she came in and chatted with Harvey for a bit. But you know her. She's friendly to everyone."

"Did she ever talk to you about going to Peru?" Logan asked.

Annie cocked her head and stared at the wall. "You know, she never did. That's why I found the rumors strange."

Logan placed his elbows on the table. "What do you mean, rumors?"

"I think one of the guys on the rodeo board told me." Annie pursed her lips. "But I can't remember for sure."

Izzie ran a finger around the rim of her cup. "I'm sure you hear a lot." Izzie's gaze skimmed the crowd. "What are people saying about Lisa's disappearance?"

"Some think something bad happened to her. Others believe she went of her own free will." Annie shrugged. "I don't believe she up and left. That's not like her."

"Thanks, Annie."

"I'm sorry I couldn't help more. Do you think she's okay?"

Izzie rested her hand on top of Annie's. "I hope so."

Annie nodded. "If that's all, I need to get back to work."

"Thank you for taking the time to talk with us." Logan smiled.

"Anytime." Annie returned to her employees and customers.

Logan grabbed his coffee and rested against the back of his seat. "What do you think?"

"Lisa didn't go to Peru like the text message from her suggested. Someone tried to make it look that way."

"Well, duh. *I* think that and so do you." He massaged his temples. "What do you think about the information you've gathered so far?"

"There's not much to go on. And that worries me. My hope is that the coroner finds evidence when he examines Carrie Norton." Izzie retrieved her phone and shot off a text to her part-time deputy brother. "I asked Daniel to meet us at the sheriff's office in an hour so the three of us can reexamine what I do have. That should give him time to finish his ranch chores."

"I'd love to see what you've put together. I'd also like more information about Grey and Harvey. Not to mention that bronc rider Isaac Sample."

"You think it's someone she dated?" Izzie had considered it but had nothing to lead her to a conclusion either way. But it made the most sense that whoever took Lisa was familiar with her.

Logan shrugged. "I honestly don't know. But it's worth a shot."

Izzie scooted back. "I can fill you in on a lot about them, but let's head to my office, and you can start reading those files."

"I like that plan." Logan stood and snapped his fingers. Shadow appeared from under the table and took his position next to Logan. "After you."

She stood, pushed in her chair and ambled toward the door. "I keep running my last conversation with Lisa through my head. I wish I could latch on to something that would give us a clue to where she is."

"Same."

They strolled to the truck, and Logan held the passenger door open for her.

Boot on the running board, she hefted herself onto the seat. "I'm doing my best to find her."

"That's all I can ask for." He shut her door and moved to the driver's side. Shadow jumped into the back seat and lay down.

Her phone rang. "Sheriff Sinclair."

"Hey, Sheriff." Her administrative assistant greeted her.

"Hi, Cory. What's up?"

"I received a call about an abandoned truck about ten miles outside of town."

"Okay?"

"Sheriff, the description matches Lisa Russell's. I thought you'd like to know."

Izzie straightened in the seat. “Who called it in?”

“It was anonymous. I didn’t recognize the voice. Which is weird for me around these parts.”

“I agree. You seem to know everyone in the county and then some.”

“You want me to put Deputy McGregor on it?”

“No. Don’t bother Phil. I’ll take this one myself.”

“Got it. I’ll send you the coordinates.”

Izzie hung up and texted Daniel not to rush to the office.

Logan shifted to face her. “May I ask what that was about?”

“Cory received an anonymous tip about an abandoned truck fitting the description of Lisa’s.”

He started the engine. “Where to?”

She gave him the GPS coordinates. He punched them into his phone and peeled out of the parking lot.

“We can’t find her if you wreck.”

He eased up on the accelerator. “Sorry.”

“I get it. I do. But we have to be smart about this.”

Logan’s jaw twitched.

Izzie stared out the window, twisting her hands together. Would she find Lisa’s body like she had Carrie’s last night?

A left turn switched from the paved highway to a dirt path. When Cory told Izzie about the abandoned truck, she hadn’t envisioned the vehicle hidden on an obscure back road. She should have realized by the coordinates Cory had given her. She had to get it together.

Two months of work and her only discovery was that two barrel racers had gone missing over the past year and a half—and one had turned up dead. Her foot bounced, jiggling her knee as her ex, Will’s words slammed into her gut like a punch. *You don’t deserve that badge you’re wearing. You’re clueless. How do you expect to solve crimes or hold your own against a criminal? You’re a weak—worthless—officer.* Maybe she should turn over the investigation into Lisa's disappearance to Daniel. She couldn't mess up this case. A quiet whimper escaped.

"Izzie?" Logan's concerned voice made her cringe.

"I'm good. Just thinking." About her incompetence. No. Izzie refused to allow Will's hateful words to affect her ability to find her friend. She wouldn't let him interfere by making her question her skills as an investigator. Straightening in her seat, she scanned the woods on both sides of the road and watched the GPS.

"We're getting close." The dirt road had little to no shoulder, with the ditch beyond rising to thick woods on either side, reminding her of where she'd found Carrie's body last night.

Shadow stuck his head over the seat, laid it on her shoulder and panted in her ear.

"He's trying to help," Logan said as he slowed the vehicle to a crawl.

Uncertain whether he meant help with her nervous energy or with the search for Lisa's truck, either way, she'd accept the dog's comfort. Izzie scratched the side of Shadow's head but never took her eyes off the tree line. The reported truck had to be somewhere nearby. "Shadow's been a good companion for you since the bombing, hasn't he?"

"More than you'll ever know. I hadn't realized I needed a service dog. I'm glad my commander insisted I take Shadow." Logan took a deep breath. "We should see the truck anytime."

A deep depression in the brush along the side of the road caught Izzie's attention. "There." She pointed to her right. A tailgate, barely visible, some twenty feet behind tangled limbs, sat between two elm trees surrounded by cedars and oaks, making it difficult to see the vehicle.

Logan stopped and rested his wrist on the steering wheel. "How did anyone find this? Better yet, how did they get a description of it?"

"No idea. It's tucked in there. I wouldn't have spotted it if we weren't looking for it." She examined the area. "A hunter, maybe?"

"Then why not give your admin assistant a name?"

"Isn't that the question of the day?" Izzie gripped the door handle. "Come on. There may be evidence to point us in the right direction." She hoped one of those clues wouldn't be Lisa's body. She hadn't allowed herself to think the worst since Lisa went missing and refused to now. Lisa was alive. She had to be.

"What if—"

"No. Just no. She is not in there." Izzie opened her door, unwilling to continue the conversation. She met Logan and Shadow at the front of his vehicle. The man had two flashlights in his hand and offered her one. "Thanks."

"How do you want to do this?"

She appreciated his confidence in her. "I suggest a wide perimeter and spiral our way in. But I'll accept any suggestions you have, Mr. Navy SEAL."

The corner of his mouth tipped upward. "Now you sound like a little sister. And believe me, I've never viewed you that way."

Izzie swallowed—hard. Memories of him asking her out flooded her mind. As did her immediate no to his offer. She'd hurt his feelings, but at the time, her father's betrayal had wrapped her in so much heartache that she hadn't noticed the sting of her words until Lisa pointed out her mistake.

"Forget I said anything." He patted Shadow's head. "You go first. Shadow and I will follow your lead."

An apology sat on her lips, but unable to bring herself to say it, she nodded. Her focus had to remain on finding Lisa, not teenage regret.

The sun shone brightly, and the humid warmth from the thick foliage formed sweat droplets that trickled down her back and beaded on her forehead. She swung the flashlight side to side across the ground, illuminating the underbrush where the daylight didn't penetrate. A twisted ankle or broken leg wasn't out of the realm of possibilities.

Izzie plodded through the tangled roots and limbs. She had no intention of bringing up the past, but the silent mental struggle about her friend was killing her. Time for something other than the worst-case scenarios inundating her thoughts.

"Lisa has kept me up-to-date about your adventures. I know you're a navy SEAL. And you said you're on terminal leave after the incident where you injured your shoulder and hip. I guess I want to know if you're okay." She'd seen him massage his shoulder and noticed his slight limp as he walked, so his physical injuries continued to bother him. But her interest centered on the psychological ones.

Logan remained quiet for several minutes as they circled the truck, continuing to move closer, looking for evidence. "My shoulder still gives me fits. And my hip hasn't completely healed. The bruising went deep, and I strained the muscles, but thankfully no bones broke. The concussion symptoms have gone. I'm clear on that front."

"And your PTSD?"

He stumbled and stared at her.

"Logan. I might not be special forces or have experienced combat. But I'm not stupid either. PTSD is brutal. It doesn't happen to just military personnel. Anyone can suffer from it."

He narrowed his gaze. "It sounds like you're speaking from experience."

Yeah, but he didn't need to know about the drug deal she'd walked in on as a rookie cop that about cost her her life. Izzie shrugged. "So, I ask again. How are you *really* doing?"

"I have my moments, but Shadow is good at his job. He keeps me grounded." The dog pressed against Logan's leg, in tune with his owner. "I have nightmares and get itchy around explosives."

"That's understandable." She visually examined the truck from where they stood. Her stomach plummeted. "Logan?"

He closed his eyes and exhaled, before locking his gaze onto her. "I see it."

"It's Lisa's."

He nodded. "I recognize the Marshall County Rodeo sticker in the back window, along with the Rollins Chili Cook-Off one."

"Let me call in confirmation we found her truck. Then we'll look for evidence in and on the vehicle." Izzie slid her phone from her pocket, placed a call to Cory, then dialed Daniel's number.

"Hey, sis, what's up?" A calf bawled in the background.

"Are you still at the ranch?"

"Yup. I'm out here rolling around in the pasture, playing with the cows." He laughed. "Nah. I promised our ranch hand, Garrett, I'd count cows this morning. Just finished. I'm heading to the office as soon as I change clothes."

"I suggest you nix the change of clothes part and get to my location A-SAP."

"What's going on?" Her rarely serious brother switched to all business.

"Logan and I found Lisa's truck. We plan to examine it as soon as I get off the phone. Unless we find Lisa inside, there's no more doubt about her disappearance. We'll officially have a missing person's case."

Logan blanched.

Sorry. She mouthed. She didn't mean to sound so blunt.

"I'm on my way." Daniel hung up.

"I'm truly sorry about that, Logan. I wasn't thinking."

"It's okay. You spoke the truth." Logan sighed. "I have to be ready for the worst."

Izzie jerked her head toward the truck. "As long as she's not in there, there's still hope. Come on. We have work to do."

While walking the perimeter, she and Logan had worked

together as a team like they'd partnered for years. As they advanced on the truck with caution, Shadow pushed against Logan's leg and whined.

"Thanks, Buddy." Logan patted the dog's head.

"Let me look first, just in case." Izzie dreaded the next step.

"No." He shook his head. "I need to know if she's in there."

"If you're sure."

"I am. You check the cab, and I'll look in the truck bed."

Izzie skirted the truck to the passenger's side, questioning her decision to give him permission for a first look. Dread settled in her belly. She peered through the window and released the breath she hadn't known she'd held. "She's not in here."

"She's not back here either." Logan's shoulders drooped in relief.

"Let's search the truck. Start with a visual, then we'll take pictures. Since I don't have an evidence kit, after we finish, we'll call the crime scene tech. Here." She retrieved two pairs of nitrile gloves that she'd shoved in her pocket and tossed him a set.

He caught the gloves, put them on and opened the driver's door. He leaned on the seat. His flashlight illuminated the floorboard while Izzie searched from the passenger's side.

Shadow paced in a circle, whimpering.

She lifted her gaze to Logan. "What's up with him?"

"I don't know. Maybe he senses our tension."

She opened the glove box and flipped through the items. Nothing. The dog barked. "Man, he's not happy about something."

Logan rested his forearms on the seat. His gaze met hers. "He's probably upset he can't help."

"He's a sweetie. I'm glad you have him. He seems to have great instincts. If he hadn't warned us about the natural gas, we might not have gotten out in time."

"I think most dogs have a sixth sense."

Her neck prickled. *Instincts. Shadow sensed something.* They hadn't checked for Lisa's body under the truck. Her insides twisted. She lay on her belly and ran the light under the truck. No Lisa. Her entire being turned to jelly at the immense relief. The beam of her flashlight caught something red. She flipped to her back, wormed her way under the vehicle and swept the undercarriage.

"What are you doing?" Logan's voice filtered down from the cab.

Her lungs seized. "Logan, don't move."

"Copy that. What's going on?"

"There might be a reason Shadow is acting weird." The world became eerily silent.

"You found her?" The catch in Logan's voice was unmistakable.

"No. I found your other worst nightmare."

Logan released a long stream of air. "Explosives."

"Affirmative."

"And?"

"Counting down. Four minutes and forty-three seconds left."

"Get out from under there."

"On it." She wiggled out. Peering through the passenger side, she stared at him. "Now what?"

"I'm going to try and disarm it." Sweat beaded on his upper lip, and his hands trembled. "But I don't know if it was triggered by the doors or if it's the pressure I'm applying to the driver's seat."

She closed her eyes. She hadn't thought of that. "Let's switch places."

"That might not be possible."

"We have to try. If not, the only solid lead we have into Lisa's disappearance will be blown to smithereens. Not to mention us." Her stomach sank at the possibility of losing evidence.

"Thanks for that visual."

"Sorry." She grimaced.

"Come around. I don't think it will explode. If it's a pressure plate, it would've gone off with all my movement."

"Doesn't matter. I'm changing places with you until you examine the bomb." Izzie's heart pounded like a stampede of cattle. She leaned in on the seat while Logan eased off. "I've got this. Go figure out how to disarm that thing." She swallowed and fought back the tears. She had to be tough. As the sheriff of Marshall County, she couldn't allow weakness. But if there were ever a time, now would be it.

Of all the places in the world that Logan thought he'd face another explosive, Rollins, Texas, wasn't one of them. His gut twisted. A storm of indecision warred inside. Every muscle screamed to refuse Izzie's demand to switch places, but he had to confirm whether or not the person who'd lured them to Lisa's truck had used a pressure plate. His gut said no—but could he trust that anymore? The possibility was the only reason he hadn't shouted at her to run. If someone else died on his watch…he'd crumble beneath the weight of the guilt. Yeah, like he hadn't already. Survivor's guilt, according to the navy shrink. Who was he to argue that point since the doctor had hit the target?

Logan held his breath as he lifted from where he lay across the driver's seat and backed away, switching places with Izzie. When the truck didn't explode, he exhaled. "I'll go check things out and see what I can do. But if I tell you to run, you do it without question."

She glared at him. "I'm not stupid."

"Right. Like a sane person would lay on top of an explosive device."

"What does that say about someone who defuses them?" She raised an eyebrow, challenging him to contradict her.

"We'll pick this conversation up later. We're running out of time." His pulse hammered as he lowered himself to the dirt. Shoving away the suffocating weight of the memories surrounding his last mission, he shimmied under the engine compartment. His light flicked over the device, and his stomach clenched.

Three and a half minutes.

"Well?" Izzie asked.

"Give me a second."

The red numbers flashed. Each tick hammered against his ribs.

He traced the wires with his finger from the detonator to the C-4 attached to the undercarriage and studied the setup. In his peripheral vision, the timer continued to tick down. The red numbers flashed to the next in a hypnotic rhythm. Whoever planted the bomb knew what they were doing. The connections he had to examine were nestled deep behind the engine. He wormed to a different position for a better view. His gut tightened. If he had his tools—if he had more time—he could stop it. He had neither. Reality had a way of sucker-punching a person.

The guy who'd planted the device hadn't used a pressure plate, of that he was confident—kind of—maybe. What if he'd come to the wrong conclusion? He'd lose Izzie and Shadow.

God, help me with this? I'm second-guessing everything.

Logan squeezed his eyes shut. His choice made. "You can lift off the seat. It's not a pressure plate." The display read two minutes. Allowing the evidence that might help find his sister to be destroyed raked across his heart, but Izzie's, Shadow's and his lives were at stake.

Izzie's upside-down face appeared. "Did you disarm it?"

He wiggled from beneath the truck, grabbed the fender and pulled to a stand. His hip protested the movement. "I can't do it in time. We have to get out of here. I want you to sprint to my truck as fast as you can. Duck down behind the front tire and cover your head."

Her eyes widened. "You're coming too, right?"

"I'll be right behind you. I promise." His internal timer nudged him to move. One minute remained. "Go."

Izzie took off.

"Shadow, come." Logan's heart pounded as he tore off after her. Izzie aimed for the front. He could hear the tick of time in his head—louder than his own breath. He slid behind the vehicle a few seconds after her.

Thirty seconds.

Shadow whined and curled on his lap. Logan leaned over the dog, shielding as much of his furry friend as possible.

Fifteen seconds.

He braced for the one thing he never wanted to experience again.

Ten.

Nine.

Logan's head whirled.

Three.

Two.

The blast roared with a concussive wave that rattled his bones. The ground shook, and debris rained down. But it was the dust that choked him. Thick. Suffocating. Filling his throat and lungs. He convulsed with a cough and gasped. But the air wouldn't come.

Shadow barked, and a wet tongue trailed up his cheek.

Why couldn't he breathe?

God, please. I have to protect Izzie.

His vision narrowed, and a dark tunnel snuffed out the light.

FOUR

Small particles of debris rained down around Izzie. Her ears rang, and she shook from the ground-rattling blast. The truck had protected her from the worst of the explosion. She slapped her hands over her ears, hoping the ringing would stop. She staggered to her feet and peered over the edge of the hood. Flames slithered upward, and thick, black smoke billowed into the sky. A sharp, bitter metallic tang added a nauseating layer to the air. Any potential evidence of Lisa's whereabouts—gone.

Hands trembling, she slid her phone from her pocket. It took several attempts to hit Daniel's number. Since she couldn't hear at the moment, she watched for the call to connect. When the counter on the screen started, she brought it to her ear. "Send the volunteer fire department and deputies to my location." She worried the fire would spread through the woods, but thankfully they'd had a wet spring, so it shouldn't expand too quickly.

She leaned against the vehicle. The movement sent her world spinning. She placed her hand on her forehead, willing the motion to stop.

"Izzie!"

She blinked. Daniel must be yelling if she'd heard her name. "Alive but need help." She glanced at Logan and Shadow. The dog nudged Logan's chin and licked his cheek, but Logan didn't move. His eyes had glossed over, and he stared straight ahead.

"Gotta go." Izzie hung up, no idea if her brother was talking or not. She had to help Logan.

The phone returned to her pocket, she stumbled the short distance to Logan's side and dropped next to him. "Logan?" She ran a hand over Shadow's head. The poor thing shivered beneath her touch. "It's okay, boy. You're doing good helping your dad."

Both man and dog appeared shaken. But Shadow focused on his task. Logan's sightless gaze worried her. She cupped the man's cheek. "Logan, can you hear me?" Well, duh. If his ears were ringing as much as hers, probably not. Although, the intensity had died down a bit. She could actually make out sounds. Scooting closer, she placed her mouth next to his ear. "We're safe. The truck is gone, but you saved Shadow and me."

She looked for any signs he'd heard her. The gut-wrenching truth slammed into her. The explosion had triggered him, and by the looks of it, Logan had tumbled back to his last mission.

"Did you hear me? You saved us. We're alive." Remembering she had divine backup, she tipped her face to the sky. *God, I could really use Your help here.*

Shadow settled at the rhythmic stroke of her hand. However, the dog whined and nudged Logan.

"You're worrying Shadow." And me. "You're in Rollins, Texas, not some place overseas. You protected us."

Logan snatched her wrist. His eyes darted around, as if searching for context or danger. She wasn't sure which. He focused on her face. "Izzie?"

Relief soaked into every pore of her body. She'd have dropped to the ground if she hadn't already been there. "Yes. It's me. Shadow too. He's worried about you."

The recollection of events was evident on his face. He loosened his grip and ran his gaze over her and Shadow. "You're both okay? No injuries?"

She shrugged. “Other than the annoying hum in my ears, I’m not hurt. How about you?”

The time it took for him to process her question concerned her.

“I’m good.” He dropped his chin, and his shoulders sagged. “Sorry I spaced out on you.”

“You have nothing to apologize for.”

“The evidence…” His words trailed off.

“It’s gone, but we’ll figure it out. I promise.” Maybe she shouldn’t have made that bold vow, but his dejected look shredded her heart.

An engine roared in the distance. Izzie jerked her gaze to the road. “Help is coming.” She pointed at Daniel’s truck speeding toward them.

Logan twisted. “We survived the bomb only to be run over by your brother if he doesn’t slow down.”

Izzie inhaled and relaxed. Logan had shaken off the effects of what she assumed was a flashback or a mental blackout.

The vehicle skidded to a stop. Daniel jumped out and sprinted toward them. “Izzie! Logan!”

Logan pressed a hand to the back panel of his truck and stood. Shadow plastered himself to Logan’s side. “We’re good, but Lisa’s truck is DOA.”

Daniel gripped Logan’s shoulder. “Are you sure you’re okay?”

“Yes.”

“Izzie?”

“I’m fine.” She held out her arms, proving there weren’t any injuries. Okay, bad idea. She had a few scrapes and minor cuts, but her brother didn’t seem to notice.

Daniel enveloped her in a hug. “Don’t scare me like that again.”

She melted in her brother’s arms. “I had no idea the truck would be rigged to explode.”

He pulled back and scrunched his nose, confused. "I meant not answering my questions on the call."

"Oh, that. The blast had my ears ringing to the point that I couldn't hear."

Her brother took a step back and scanned the scene. His classic fun-loving self was nonexistent. "I think I need a rundown of what happened."

Izzie swallowed the sob that threatened to escape. She had to pull it together. "We received an abandoned truck report, and Logan and I volunteered to investigate."

"How? Who? Why?" Daniel shot off the questions faster than a weapon on the shooting range.

"An anonymous call came in. Cory couldn't identify the voice. As for why I took the assignment, the description sounded like Lisa's truck."

Daniel glanced at the pile of burning metal. "Was it?"

She nodded.

"The explosive attached to the undercarriage of the truck says someone set us up." Logan straightened, appearing a little more settled after his trip down memory lane.

"How would the person know you'd take the callout?" Daniel crossed his arms and arched an eyebrow.

"Random?" Logan offered.

"That doesn't make sense. I hadn't discovered the whereabouts of Lisa's truck. Why not hide it completely out of sight or destroy it so it's never found?" Her gaze drifted to the burning shell of Lisa's vehicle. "Someone didn't pass by this area for two months then suddenly saw it."

"Okay, fine. So, it wasn't random. That takes us back to why, and how did he know it would be you?" The color in Logan's cheeks had returned.

"Stick a pin in that." Daniel motioned for them to join him at his truck. He lowered the tailgate. "Have a seat before the two of you fall down and tell me what happened."

The story spilled out over the next few minutes. Sirens echoed off the trees, signaling the volunteer fire department and her deputies had dispatched to her location. Moments later, the fire truck rolled to a stop. Four men jumped out and went to work putting out the blaze before it moved further into the woods.

She and Logan sat on the tailgate and gave their statement to her deputy Jackie Bennett.

The adrenaline faded, and Izzie's energy waned. The last twenty-four hours had taken its toll.

Logan squeezed her hand. "As much as I want to stick around to see if your deputies find any evidence as to who took Lisa or tried to blow us up, I vote we get out of here."

Her gaze landed on their entwined fingers. Faint scars marred the back of his hands and forearms. A reminder of his brush with death, no doubt. Izzie lifted her gaze—instantly drawn into the depths of his brown eyes. This was her best friend's twin brother. The man she'd told no years ago. So why had her heart chosen that moment to begin melting from the frozen, loveless organ Will claimed it to be?

Logan hadn't planned to come to Izzie's family ranch, but Daniel insisted. When his friend pulled the mom card for Izzie and the veterinarian one for Shadow, he'd given in. Besides, he'd have to get a hotel room until the fire department cleared Lisa's house.

He sat on the couch in the living room at Stone Creek Ranch and ran his hand over the soft, cool leather. Freed from his duties, Shadow lay on a makeshift bed of folded blankets next to him on the floor. A ruckus of voices and laughter filtered in from the kitchen. He and Lisa had spent a ton of time on the ranch growing up—Lisa visiting Izzie, and Logan tagging along like a stray puppy. Didn't that just describe his life—until he joined the navy and became a SEAL. He'd found his purpose until an explosion shattered that dream. He'd intended to be a lifer, but God had other plans. Logan wished he knew why. But he trusted God, so here he sat, with his sister missing and a service dog for his PTSD at his feet.

"Well, aren't you the sweetest thing?" Izzie's sister, Payton Sinclair, waltzed in the room and aimed herself toward Shadow. She kneeled and lavished the dog with love. Her hands smoothed over the canine, and she kissed his nose. With a groan of pleasure, Shadow rolled over and exposed his belly. Payton looked up. "What's his name?"

"It's good to see you again, Payton. And to answer your question, Shadow."

"Sorry about that. I'm good with animals." She shrugged. "People not so much."

That wasn't what he remembered about the youngest Sinclair sibling. The girl he'd known had been outgoing. Now, she appeared as though she'd lived through immense pain. A familiar feeling for him, which made it easier to spot in others.

Payton's hand never stopped scratching the dog's belly. "I heard he's a service dog."

Logan nodded. "His owner died about the time I came back to the States. I needed him as much as he needed me. He and I are best buds."

"Well, let me check him out for you then."

"I'd appreciate that."

Payton retrieved her vet bag from by the front door and went to work.

"I see our resident animal lover came to the rescue." Izzie joined him on the couch. She handed him a glass of iced tea and kept one for herself.

"That's Dr. Sinclair to you, sis." She gave Izzie a cheesy grin that didn't quite reach her eyes. Something was definitely up there, but he wouldn't pry. He'd stayed away from his hometown too long. A practical stranger to those he'd grown up with.

Izzie stuck her tongue out at her younger sister and crossed her eyes.

And why did he find the juvenile act so adorable? *Slow your roll, dude. Remember, it's your sister's best friend who's already rejected you.* Shadow's low groan of pleasure shifted Logan's attention to Payton as she cared for Shadow, but he spoke to Izzie. "Anything from Daniel?"

"He's on his way. Said he had an update, but nothing significant." She took a sip. "Either way, I want to lay out all the information we have. See if we can find the missing piece that solves the mystery and helps us find Lisa." The *before it's too late* was implied. "He's in good hands." Izzie gestured toward Payton with her glass. "She's the best vet around these parts."

"I can see that."

"Oh, please. I'm not doing much." Payton rolled her eyes.

"You don't understand. Shadow is easygoing, but he hates going to the vet. And right now, he appears to be loving you." A smile tugged on the corner of Logan's mouth. His furry friend no longer whimpered after the explosion.

"Then I'll take that as a compliment." Payton squished Shadow's face in between her hands. "Isn't that right, you cute little thing?"

Shadow's tongue peeked out of his mouth and then struck out and licked Payton.

Payton laughed and fell over. The pair played on the floor.

"It's good to see her happy," Izzie whispered.

He jerked his gaze to hers. "She hasn't been?"

Izzie shrugged. "We've noticed she's not as bubbly as she used to be, but she refuses to tell us anything."

"I hope she'll confide in one of you."

"Me too, but she hasn't yet." Izzie stared at her sister, who snuggled with Shadow on the floor. "She's keeping a secret. And my sheriff brain goes to the worse possible scenarios."

"Don't go to those dark places until you know for sure. She'll tell you when she's ready." Logan understood. It had taken weeks before he'd spoken while meeting with the military-provided therapist. They'd had long sessions of silence during his hospital stay until he finally hit the wall and spilled his guts to the woman.

"I hope so." The distant look in Izzie's eyes returned.

He had a nagging feeling, not for the first time, that Izzie held on to her own secret.

Daniel burst into the room. "I know you missed me, but don't worry. I'm here." The man's grin lit up his face.

"Sit down, you goof." Izzie motioned to the recliner.

Daniel plopped onto the chair. "What did I miss?"

"Nothing." Payton sat cross-legged with Shadow in her lap. Not exactly a good fit with the dog's size. The crazy mutt thought he was a lapdog. "Do I need to leave?"

Izzie shook her head. "You're fine. Yes, it's an investigation, but let's be honest. No matter how hard I try to keep things confidential, the information will spread through town faster than a wildfire in a Texas drought."

"Gotta love a small town." Logan hadn't missed that aspect of Rollins. Your business was everyone's business. The community didn't mean any harm by it. Just the reality of a close-knit town.

Izzie shifted to face Daniel. "What did you find out?"

"With the reminder that most of the findings are preliminary, I can say for certain that the truck was Lisa's. After the firefighters put out the blaze, we matched the VIN number to her DMV records. For how long it sat in the woods, I'm not sure. Shane Carter's house is about three miles down that road. He travels past that area a lot. He said he never saw it. Granted, he's eighty-five, but still."

Izzie's brow arched. "I'll put his eighty-five-year-old observation abilities up against the best detectives in Texas. That man is sharp."

"That's true." Daniel reclined and clasped his hands over his stomach. "Anyhoo, that leaves us without a timeline for when our bad guy abandoned the truck there."

Logan rubbed his forehead. The pressure inside his skull increased with the conversation. "I wish we could do better."

"Sorry, man. I promise we'll keep at it." Daniel continued with his update. "The explosives were—"

"C-4 with a detonator attached to a timer."

Daniel pointed at him. "What the man said. Remember this is all preliminary. But Jackie found pieces of the device twenty feet from the blast. She's taking them to the lab in Lackard. She knows a guy who specializes in explosives."

"Any evidence of what triggered the device?"

"As if I'd know what that would look like, bomb guy." Daniel rolled his eyes.

"The way it all went down, my guess is that the bomb was rigged with a pressure-sensitive trigger, hidden within the truck's door mechanism. When I opened the door, it completed the circuit, activating the timer. But why have the delay and not ignite it immediately?"

Daniel's eyes widened, and the comical expression almost made Logan laugh. "Dude, was there any English in that statement?"

"At this point, I don't care how the delay happened. That timer saved our lives." Izzie narrowed her gaze, challenging him and Daniel to disagree.

Daniel lifted his hands, palms up. "She has a valid argument."

"For which I'm grateful. I just wish I could have disarmed it." He'd failed on that part, but at least they'd survived.

"That's not on you." Izzie's no-nonsense tone yanked him from falling into the pit of guilt. "Now that we established that, keep going, Daniel."

"Jackie, Phil and Vince aren't going to stop examining the

area or the remains of the truck until they have answers." Daniel flipped the footrest down and leaned forward. "Now, let's talk about your attack."

"What about it?" Izzie asked.

"Come on. I know you're a better investigator than that."

Izzie flinched.

Logan noticed but he didn't think Daniel had, or the man would have latched on to it.

"What are you thinking?" Logan steered the conversation back in Daniel's direction.

"Stay with me here. Lisa left town two months ago, except we didn't have solid proof it wasn't of her own free will. Izzie doesn't believe the text she received from Lisa the next day and gets a burr under her saddle. She starts asking questions and looking into other missing women in the region. Then you, Logan, call Izzie a couple days back. Last night, Izzie's attacked and almost killed while responding to the discovery of a dead body. Who, I might add, is one of the women she has a file on. The coroner confirmed it was Carrie Norton's body thirty minutes ago. After you leave the scene, there's an odd gas leak at Lisa's house. One that RFD is investigating. I talked with the fire captain, and he's agreed to look at it with a suspicious eye. Add to that, a little while ago, the two of you came close to being blown to bits. If you ask me, it all adds up to something shady."

"Thanks for that visual, bro," Izzie huffed. "You're implying that someone doesn't want me poking around into Lisa's whereabouts, and that person is willing to eliminate me?"

"See, you *can* be taught." Daniel grinned.

Logan didn't miss the slight droop in Izzie's shoulders. Her reactions bothered him. "Just thinking out loud here. If Lisa's disappearance is related to the two other women, what if they aren't the only ones?"

Daniel's eyes popped to his. "As in there might be more that we don't know about?"

"It's possible." He hated to bring it up, but the nagging voice in his head wouldn't let it go.

Payton, who had stayed silent throughout the discussion, kissed his dog on the nose and padded from the room without a word.

Izzie pushed from the couch. Her arms wrapped her middle as if holding herself together. Shadow's black eyes tracked her as she paced the living room. "If what you are suggesting is true…" Her words trailed off.

Daniel steepled his fingers and tapped his chin. "Maybe."

Logan reached behind the couch and clasped her wrist as she walked by. A twinge zipped through his shoulder. He bit back the grimace. "Izzie, it doesn't mean you failed. Only that people around these potential victims hadn't noticed."

She glanced at his fingers. Her hand slid from his light grip and rolled to hold his hand. "If that's the case, who hasn't been seen in the past year or so, even if they had a reason to leave?"

The room grew silent. Logan had nothing to add since he hadn't returned home in years. The navy controlled his life. And his missions as a SEAL—his top priority. He didn't regret his service to his country. But his lack of connection to his hometown and his childhood friends, not to mention his sister, bothered him.

Daniel snapped his fingers. "The only woman I know that I haven't seen in over a year is Whitney Morris."

"The barrel racer who left for home in Montana after her breakup with Chase Fowler?" Izzie asked.

"Yup. I remember talking with Chase afterward. He said they had an argument. The next day he found a note that she never wanted to see him again and that she'd packed up and gone home to Montana."

"Did he mention what they argued about?" Izzie stared at Daniel.

"Not really. He said it was stupid, and it shocked him that

she up and left. Especially after she rode her personal record the night before." Daniel filled in the blanks.

Logan motioned for Izzie to come sit beside him. She released his hand and skirted the couch. He instantly missed the connection between them. His heart wanted something it couldn't have. He had to remember that.

"Could the abductor have left the note for her boyfriend, similar to the text supposedly from Lisa?" The room grew quiet. Logan knew of one way to find out. "May I suggest we contact Whitney's parents and confirm she made it home?"

Izzie scowled.

"Sorry, I didn't mean to overstep."

"You didn't."

"Then why the growly face?" Daniel asked.

"If, and that's a big if, Whitney is missing, then there's a common denominator."

Daniel rolled his eyes. "Please, for the love of everything, don't math on me."

"You dork." Izzie shook her head. "Why did I ever hire you?"

"Because you love me." Daniel flashed his pearly whites.

Logan covered his mouth to hide his smile. Some things never changed. And the banter between these two was one of them. Yet again, maybe Daniel *had* recognized Izzie's reaction early. His friend had a way of lightening the mood under the most serious of circumstances.

"What were you going to say, Izzie?" he asked to bring them back on track.

"All four women are barrel racers who disappeared after competing in a rodeo."

"I'll deep dive into missing persons and ask around the rodeo scene about barrel racers who unexpectedly moved from the region."

"Thanks, Daniel. But if this guy snatched multiple women, don't limit it to our region. Put feelers throughout Texas and the surrounding states. I don't want to make assumptions about location. Logan and I will call Whitney's parents, and depending on what we find out, we'll go from there."

"I want to add that Izzie needs to be extra cautious. Whoever is out there somehow knows her movements, and he has her in his crosshairs..." Logan let the statement die out. He'd let his twin sister down. He refused to do the same for Izzie.

FIVE

Church and family lunch on Sunday was a normal occurrence for Izzie, but Logan sitting beside her during the service—a complete surprise. The man's faith hadn't existed back in the day. Lisa, on the other hand, had flourished under her faith. One of the reasons her text message about the mission trip to Peru wasn't completely off the rails. But it hadn't fooled Izzie.

Lunch finished, Izzie pulled her SUV away from the ranch house and headed to the sheriff's office. Sunday was normally her day off, but with the discovery of Carrie Norton's body and Lisa's truck, she couldn't afford to wait.

Shadow had claimed the back seat and sprawled out like he owned it. She snuck a peek at the man sitting next to her. Logan had changed over the years. Physically stronger. More confident. Nothing major, except for his apparent belief in God.

A few minutes of quiet later, Izzie couldn't help herself. "Okay, spill."

Logan twisted and tilted his head. "What are you talking about?"

Might as well say it like it is. "I've never seen you willingly grace the door of a church."

"Oh, that." He puffed out a breath. "Life experiences tend to change people."

"Let me guess." She glanced at him then back to the road. "A foxhole conversion?"

"Something like that." He shifted and stared out the passenger window.

"Go on. I'd like to hear how you and God became friends."

He released a long breath. "My team was sent to a very intense place." A sly smile crossed his lips. "Sorry, classified."

She rolled her eyes. "Of course it is. Go on, Mr. Team Guy."

"We were pinned down. Extraction fifteen minutes out. We didn't have that long. God became very real in those moments. I couldn't deny His existence any longer, so He and I had a chat." He lifted a shaky hand and smoothed it over his mouth.

"Obviously you made it out, but what happened?"

Shadow popped his head over the seat and laid it against Logan's neck.

Logan leaned into his dog and ran a hand over the animal's neck. "Remember Shadrach, Meshach and Abednego and the fiery furnace?"

"What kid raised in the church doesn't?" She'd feared being trapped in fires for weeks after that Sunday school lesson.

"Right. Well, that's the best description I can come up with. I prayed for forgiveness then I prayed hard for us to make it out of there alive." His voice cracked on the last words.

Izzie gave him a moment to gather himself and checked her mirrors. Their brainstorming session at the ranch had put her on edge. Satisfied no one had followed them, she returned her attention to Logan. "As much as I hate the circumstances, I'm glad you found your way to God."

"Me too," he whispered.

She'd grown up in the church and had never questioned God's existence. She and Lisa had been baptized on the same day. But she'd admit, praying wasn't her first thought. It tended to be an afterthought. Something she needed to work on. "I don't understand the reference to the fiery furnace though."

"It was as if the enemy couldn't hit a target. Oh, sure, bullets struck the ground next to us, but it was like we had a shield around us. I still don't understand it. The only way to explain it is that God intervened."

Tears blurred her vision. Lisa had confided in her how scared she was for Logan when he deployed. And to find out how close he'd come to losing his life—twice that she knew of—sent a dagger into her heart. On the other hand, the situation had brought him to his knees, so to speak.

"The extraction team came screaming in and got us out of there. Once I got back to base, I tracked down our chaplain. He listened to my story and smiled. Not shocked at all. He and I became good friends that day."

"I, for one, am glad." She fought her need to reach out and hold his hand. Izzie turned on the street of the sheriff's office. "Almost there."

"What's the plan?" Logan hadn't stopped petting Shadow through the entire story about his close call with death.

"First thing is to place a call to Whitney's family. See if she ever returned to Montana. Then we'll go from there." She hadn't considered Whitney as missing. The rodeo community assumed the story about her heading home to be true—until the body in the woods.

"I'll follow your lead."

Izzie entered the parking lot and pulled into the spot that sported a Sheriff's Parking sign. The pair plus Shadow entered the building from the side door that led straight to her office, avoiding the skeleton crew on duty.

"Have a seat." She pointed to the couch she'd taken numerous lunchtime and late evening naps on over her time as sheriff. "And don't worry, Shadow can lie up there too."

"Thanks." Logan sat and patted the cushion next to him. "Come on, boy. You're allowed."

The dog eyed Logan then swung his head to her and back.

Logan laughed. "I'm telling the truth. You can join me."

Shadow's pink tongue dangled from his mouth, and the dog

hopped up. He circled the cushion, wobbling on unsteady paws, then curled up and gave a long sigh.

"He's such a drama king." Logan's hand rhythmically petted Shadow's head. The motion seemed to calm both owner and dog.

Izzie moved to her desk and powered up her computer. "Give me a minute to find Whitney's parents' information then we'll make a call."

"Take your time."

"I can multitask. Tell me more about Shadow." Izzie brought up DMV records and searched for Whitney Morris. If the young barrel racer who'd left town hadn't changed her driver's license to Texas, it'd make tracking down her family easier.

"I haven't known Shadow for all that long. His original owner died, which affected him. From what I understand, Shadow found the guy. When he first came to me, he had separation anxiety, still does to a certain extent. Which makes sense. My commander forced Shadow on me. I didn't realize how much I needed him to keep me grounded in the present. And in return, I think he needed me as well. At least that's what I'd like to believe. Shadow's chill. Other than his diva side that shows every so often, he's easygoing."

Logan chuckled.

A smile crept onto her face. She'd missed Logan's laugh. She scanned the screen, searching for a match. "What's so funny?"

He flopped the dog's ears side to side. "This crazy thing likes to ride dune buggies."

Izzie stopped working. "Say what?"

"I'm not kidding. Trent, his previous owner, loved riding dune buggies. He'd take Shadow with him. The dog had a special seat belt and goggles."

"I'd love to see that."

"Me too. Maybe one day, I'll take him." Eyes glazed over, Logan stopped petting the canine and clutched the dog tags hanging from his neck. He stared at the wall behind her. Shadow crawled onto his lap but didn't paw at him.

The man had experienced so much pain and heartache on his last mission, then to find out his twin sister had gone missing. She wondered how much more he could take.

He blinked and refocused on her. "Have you found anything?"

"Whitney's driver's license is still registered in Montana. I'm crosschecking the address as we speak." Three names popped up. She referenced the ages. "Here we go."

Logan scooted out from under Shadow and moved behind her. He read over her shoulder. "Hmm. Nancy and Max Morris. Her parents I assume."

"That's my guess. Annnnd, here is Max's phone number." She put the phone on speaker and dialed.

"Hello." An older male answered.

"May I speak with Max Morris."

"You've got him."

"Good afternoon, Mr. Morris. This is Sheriff Sinclair from Marshall County Texas."

"Sheriff. How can I help you?"

"Are you related to Whitney Morris?"

"I'm her father, why?" A slight tremor invaded his voice.

"I'm attempting to get a hold of her on a personal matter and am curious if she is home in Montana."

"No. We haven't heard from her in about a year."

"If you don't mind my asking, is there a reason she hasn't called home or visited?"

"Whit had a falling out with one of our ranch hands, Milo Stein, about two years ago. She left for Texas soon after. Her mother and I found out six months later that the man had...let's just say he's not employed on our ranch anymore."

She glanced at Logan and raised a brow. "So, she never found out you fired him?" Izzie jotted down the man's name to do a background check on later.

"She did. We talked on and off for several months then she quit calling. We're worried about her."

"Did you fill out a missing person's report?"

"We thought about it, but that girl has always drifted on the wind, if you know what I mean."

"I think I do."

"Do you know something you're not saying?"

"Not really. I'm only trying to track her down at this point."

"Please let us know if you find her. We miss her."

"You have my promise."

"Thank you, Sheriff."

"I'll be in touch." Izzie hung up. "It seems as though we now have three women missing, excluding Carrie."

"I have a bad feeling about this." Logan ran a hand over the back of his neck.

"I'm right there with ya." Izzie texted Daniel for the number of Whitney's boyfriend, Chase Fowler, and his location. If her brother didn't have it, he'd know who did. She spun and clasped Logan's hands. The man gave her confidence she'd lacked since Will's hit-and-run on her life. "I'm sorry for the reason, but I'm glad you're back in town. I've missed you."

Logan's eyes widened. "You have?"

"Of course. I've always—" Her phone buzzed, interrupting the confession of her teenage crush on him. "It's Daniel. He used his rodeo contacts to get Chase's number and location. His source says that Chase is at his house in the next county over."

"I'm up for a ride. How about you?"

"I'd rather not wait until tomorrow." Whitney had vanished, and no one seemed the wiser. Izzie wanted details.

Logan squeezed her fingers and moved to wake up Shadow, who snored on her couch. "Come on, sleepyhead. Time to go."

Shadow yawned. His black eyes fixed on Logan and grumbled.

She laughed. "He's not impressed."

"Never is when he's woken up from his beauty sleep." Logan snapped his fingers.

Shadow ambled off the couch and took his time sitting next to Logan's foot.

"Told you he was a drama king." He gestured toward the ball of black fur.

"How on earth did he make it through service dog training?"

"You'd be surprised at the shift in his mood when I give the command to w-o-r-k." He spelled out the word.

Shadow's ears mimicked antennas searching for a signal.

"Isn't he on duty all the time?"

"Yes and no. I usually put his vest on when we go out in public. That's when you'll see the change in his demeanor. He'll alert to signs of anxiety and distress even when he's not on duty like you've probably seen. But he also gets to be a normal dog at home too." He patted Shadow on the head.

"Next time we're out on the ranch, we should let him roam for a bit."

"He'd love that."

Izzie detoured to the front office to find her after-hours administrative clerk. "Hey, Sue."

"Hi, Sheriff. I didn't hear you come in."

"I snuck in the side door. I wanted to let you know I'm heading over to Briar County to interview Chase Fowler about a possible missing person's case if you need to get a hold of me."

"I'll make a note of it." Sue wrote on the pad of paper on her desk. "If you plan to work late, let me know, and I'll place a to-go order from the café."

"Thanks, Sue. Hold off on the food delivery for now. We'll see where this conversation takes us."

"You got it, Sheriff."

Logan leaned in. "I take it you work late a lot."

She shrugged. "I'm the sheriff. I have to stay on top of

things." And she had no one to go home to. So why not work long hours? Izzie faced Logan. "You ready?"

"Yup."

"Let's get moving. I'd like to talk with Chase before he moves on to another rodeo."

"Lead the way, I have your six."

Something about the way Logan ensured he'd have her back spoke to more than following her to her sheriff's department SUV—it spoke to the investigation as well. Maybe she'd read into his statement. She filed the thought away for later and headed to the parking lot with Logan and Shadow following behind her as he'd promised.

The small talk on the road to Chase's house about killed Logan. His brain had latched on to the moment they'd held hands at her desk after the phone call to Mr. Morris. For the last twelve years, he'd fought the memory of her rejecting him. But Izzie hadn't seemed repulsed at the closeness. In fact, she'd initiated it. So why had she turned him down so fast it made his head spin all those years ago?

"You okay over there?" Izzie parked the SUV in front of a small house. "You've been quiet for the last ten minutes."

"Sorry. Lost in thought." *About you and my bruised ego.* He slid from the vehicle and unclipped Shadow's seat belt harness from the back seat. The crisp scent of freshly cut grass drifting through the air reminded him of his youth on the ranch. It sure beat the dusty sand he'd inhaled during his last year with the SEALs. He'd been away from Texas far too long.

"If you don't mind, I'll ask the questions. But if something strikes you as important, feel free to jump in." She strode up the walkway like a woman on a mission.

He and Shadow hurried to catch up.

Izzie stood to the side of the door and knocked. He mimicked her stance on the opposite side. Old habits died hard and all of that.

A young man with blond hair sticking up in multiple directions answered. "May I help you?" The groggy voice indicated they'd woken him from a nap.

"We have a few questions about Whitney Morris we'd like to ask."

The man's facial expression crumpled. "Fine." He gestured to the seating on the porch. "Mind if we sit out here? I just returned from a rodeo, and my place isn't company ready."

"Not a problem." Izzie chose the love seat.

Logan lowered next to her, and Chase took the chair.

Chase rubbed his eyes. "What can I do for you?"

"How long did you and Whitney date?" Izzie asked.

"Not quite a year, I guess. I finally built up the nerve to ask her out at the final rodeo of the season two years ago. She'd won the barrel racing event that night."

Izzie's eyes widened, and she nodded. "At a major rodeo… that's worth celebrating."

"I thought so. And it gave me an excuse to ask her to dinner." Chase gave them a one-sided smile.

Logan understood the man's insecurities and hesitation. As a teen, he'd stepped well beyond his comfort zone, and Izzie had nixed him like a mission gone sideways.

Izzie leaned forward and rested her arms on her knees. "You became a couple after that?"

Chase nodded. "We hit it off. Things were going well. Or so I thought." His shoulders drooped.

"When was the last time you saw her?" Izzie asked.

"The night before she dumped me. She'd ridden a PR time, and we went to celebrate. After a late-night dinner, we had an argument about some guy that was hitting on her. I took her back to the nearby hotel where she was staying. We said goodnight but agreed to meet up in the morning. I went back to my camper at the rodeo grounds." Chase ran a hand over his messy hair.

"What happened next?" Logan knew what Daniel had said at Stone Creek Ranch but wanted to hear it firsthand.

"The next morning, I found a note under the windshield wiper of my truck. It said that we weren't working out, and she was leaving to go home to Montana." Chase narrowed his gaze. "You'd think she could have told me to my face."

Same story Daniel had told. Logan mulled over the information.

"Do you happen to still have the note?" Izzie asked.

"I planned to burn it, but I couldn't do it." Chase stared at the ceiling of the porch. "I sound lame, don't I?"

"No. I think you're a man who loved that woman and wanted to hold on to her any way possible." Logan's mouth engaged before his brain. *Projecting much?*

Izzie glanced at Logan and raised a brow.

Chase scowled. "I hate to admit it, but you're probably right."

Thank you, Chase, for bringing the attention back to you.

Izzie returned her focus to Chase. "May I see the note?"

The man shrugged. "Yeah. I suppose so. Let me grab it." Chase rose and disappeared inside.

"You don't think it's a little suspicious that he kept the note?" Izzie asked.

"I'm not willing to cross him off the list in Whitney's disappearance, but my gut says no." *Because I still have the picture of you from our last day together in my wallet.*

The screen door banged shut, and Chase held out the note. "Here."

Logan read the letter with Izzie.

She held up the paper. "I'd like to take this with me if that's okay with you."

Chase blinked. "What aren't you telling me?"

"We're trying to track her down. Not long ago, we discovered that Whitney never went home to Montana. We thought you might have more insight on her whereabouts."

Chase paced the porch. "The night before she left, we had a great evening together except for our little squabble. I had no warning that she was unhappy, let alone that she'd run off." The man spun and faced them. "You think something happened to her, don't you?"

Izzie held up a hand. "We don't know. Her name came up during a missing person's investigation. We're trying to see if there's any connection."

Chase clenched his fist. His jaw tightened. "All this time, I thought she left me. You think someone abducted her?"

A low growl rumbled from Shadow's belly. The dog sensed the anger rolling off Chase. Logan placed a hand on the dog's head, quieting him.

"Mr. Fowler, please calm down. I understand your frustration. We don't know if anything happened to Whitney. We're only trying to piece together where she went after she wrote this note." Izzie waved the paper in the air.

"All this time, I've been mad at her. Hurt that she'd leave me—leave what we had together. And now I find out that someone might have taken her." Chase rubbed the spot on his chest above his heart. "Will you please let me know what you find out?"

"Of course." Izzie stood and shook the man's hand. "If you think of anything else, please let us know."

"Thank you for sharing with us." Logan said his goodbye then led Shadow down the stairs to the SUV and clipped him in. "That was enlightening."

Izzie pulled away from the curb. "Sounds like Whitney didn't leave of her own accord."

"That's my take on it too."

"What's your first impression of Chase?"

"That the man is hurting."

"And what about Whitney and Lisa? Is there a link between

their disappearances other than barrel racing?" Izzie flipped on the turn signal and maneuvered through the neighborhood.

"Gut reaction? Yes." Logan watched the scenery turn from houses to trees lining the highway. Chase's words ran through his head like a movie reel stuck on repeat. He empathized with the man. Having the woman you loved or thought you loved turn her back on you. It stung. Not only a man's heart, but his pride as well. Logan's curiosity got the best of him. "Why did you say no to me in high school?"

Izzie's head jerked to face him. "What?" She returned her eyes to the road.

"I'd like to know why you turned me down when I asked you out." He'd lived with the uncertainty long enough. He was stronger now and could handle whatever her reasoning had been.

"What brought this up?"

"Something Chase said." He studied her while she drove. She'd matured. Experienced life. But she was still the same Izzie he remembered. "Will you please answer me?"

"You are my best friend's brother."

"That's the real reason?" He didn't buy what she was trying to sell. There had to be more to it.

Her shoulders sagged. "I'd had a crush on you for years. But you always treated me like a sister. Then Dad's affairs came to light, and Mom kicked him out. It skewed my views on relationships. When you asked me out, I wanted nothing to do with dating."

He'd forgotten how her father's betrayal had affected her. "It wasn't me?" All these years, he thought there was something about him that made her say no.

"Of course not, why would you think that?" Her gaze flicked to the rearview mirror.

He checked the side mirrors out of habit. "Even though Lisa and I are twins, I was always in her shadow. Not in a bad way. I just didn't have her self-confidence. I could pretend for a while, but I took every negative word or rejection personally. When you said no to going out, I thought there was something wrong with me."

"Oh, Logan. I never felt that way. If you'd have asked me out before all that happened, I would have said yes."

"Bad timing on my part." A huge weight lifted, and his self-esteem rose even after all these years. He sighed. "Maybe it was all for the best."

"Are you talking about the military?" She glanced at him then scanned the road and area ahead.

"Yes. The navy built up my self-esteem. After boot camp, I had something to prove to myself. I mustered the courage and requested a transfer to the SEALs. It was granted, and the real work began."

"Did you ever want to give up?"

He lifted his hand in front of the vent and felt the soft rush of air cool his fingers. A habit he'd had since childhood. "Sure. We all did at some point. I made a vow with two other guys that we wouldn't allow each other to quit." He remembered what he thought had been the most difficult day of his life and the pact between him, Rob and Chris. Came to find out that hadn't been close to the hardest.

"Did they make it as well?"

A smile formed on his face at the memory. "All three of us earned our Trident. Rob and Chris are still on the Teams."

"I assume you had women falling at your feet."

Had he heard a bit of jealousy in her tone? Would it be bad if he hoped the answer was yes? "That might be true, but I only went on one date."

She jerked her head to him. "Excuse me?"

"She..." How did he say it? "She wanted one thing, and I wasn't interested."

"Oh. I get it. I'm sorry. But why not try again?"

His gaze drifted to Izzie. The woman who'd held his heart

since his teen years. "Because of you." There. He'd said it. It had taken more courage than BUDs training to admit that.

"I…um… I'm not sure what to say."

"It's okay. It was a long time ago." Trees flew by along the side of the road. The interior of the SUV grew quiet except for Shadow's soft snores. Logan had learned patience, but his teenage broken heart reared its ugly head, and the silence tortured him. *Get it together, Russell. You're a SEAL, not an insecure kid.*

"I—" Izzie's eyes shifted to the rearview mirror and widened. "Someone's gaining on us." She hit the gas, and the SUV lurched forward.

Logan twisted and spotted the truck coming up fast.

He grabbed the handle above the door. "How long has he been back there?"

"Not long. If he followed us, he stayed out of sight until now."

The bite in Izzie's words had him wondering what he did wrong. "I believe you. It was only a question."

"Sorry." Her eyes shifted from the road to the mirror and back on repeat.

"Any idea how to lose him?"

"Not on this road. It curves around the countryside until it opens up a few miles outside of town."

"Great," Logan muttered and eyed the rifle Izzie had in her department vehicle. "Can't exactly shoot at him since he's not shooting at us."

"That would be a hard no." Izzie maneuvered around the curves at high speed, handling the SUV like a pro racecar driver.

The truck continued to gain on them. "Got any bright ideas?"

"I wish." Her attention went to her side mirror.

"Izzie, look out!"

A deer darted in front of them.

She yanked the steering wheel to the right to avoid the animal. The front tires caught on the gravel. Izzie fought to gain control, but at their current speed there was little she could do.

The SUV skidded across the shoulder of the road and into the grass, bouncing over ruts. Shadow's yelp was the last thing Logan heard before the vehicle slammed into a tree. The driver's side window shattered inward, and the air bags blew. Silence descended.

Logan blinked away the disorientation and took stock of the situation. He pushed away the air bag, coughing from the fine powder floating in the air. Izzie slumped in her seat—her door blocked by limbs and brush. He twisted to check on Shadow. The dog's tether had kept him from flying through the SUV, but his buddy lay whimpering on the seat. The crunch of tires echoed in the quiet. He peered out the rear windshield. A man stood at the side of the road. The sun's glare blocked the guy's features.

Logan froze, waiting to see what the man would do. The engine hissed, and the sickening sweet smell of radiator fluid permeated the air.

"Is he still there?" Izzie whispered. Her air bag had deflated and hung like a limp balloon in her lap.

He shifted his gaze to her. "Yes. Glad to see you're awake. Injuries? Head?"

"I think it stunned me more than anything. Scrapes and bruises from what I can tell. And of course a bloody nose." She wiped her hand under her nose, which continued to trickle blood down her upper lip.

Logan slipped his hand to the rifle locked in place at the dashboard. His fingers curled around the barrel.

Izzie snapped the lock open. "Don't be the first to fire."

He grunted. Typical rules of engagement. "Pray he leaves."

"You got it."

A few long minutes later, the rumble of a car sounded in the distance. The guy climbed into his truck and sped away.

Logan drew in air through his nose and slowly blew it out between pursed lips. "He's gone."

He heard the snap of the lock on the rifle and removed his hand from the weapon. Shadow whined. "I'm coming, boy. I'll get you out of here."

"Is he hurt?"

"I can't tell, but I'm sure the yank on his harness didn't feel good."

"I'll make sure Payton takes a look at him." Izzie fiddled with the seat belt. When it refused to release, she unclipped a small device from her keychain.

"What's that?"

"A seat belt cutter." She slid the strap into the object and sliced the nylon material in half.

"You came prepared." He pushed the release button on his seat belt. The device worked. He freed himself from the constraint. Logan pulled the handle. When the latch clicked, he pushed on the door. The thing groaned but opened. He extracted himself from the vehicle and brushed the pieces of glass from his shirt and jeans.

Izzie wiggled out from beneath the steering wheel and crawled across the front seat, swiping debris off the console and seat as she went. She stood beside him and brushed the glass from her hands. He noticed small cuts on her palms. "Why don't you get Shadow out, and I'll call for help."

He nodded. The back door creaked open, and he released the tether attached to Shadow's harness. "Come on, boy. Let's get you out of this mess."

He allowed the dog to crawl from the SUV, not wanting to aggravate any injuries the wreck might have caused. Once Shadow reached the door, Logan slid his arms under the dog and lifted him out. Placing him on the ground, he waited for Shadow to stand on his own before letting go.

Logan bent down and ran a careful hand over the dog's back.

Shadow licked his face and nuzzled into him. "I'm right here, boy." He hoped the accident didn't cause his furry friend to regress into his separation anxiety.

A siren wailed. Logan's muscles relaxed. He hadn't realized how tense he'd become.

"Daniel's on his way to pick us up. And Deputy Wagner's assigned to process the scene." Izzie stood beside him. "I also texted Payton. She'll meet us at the ranch house along with the paramedics. I don't want to stay here any longer than necessary."

"Thank you for requesting your sister." Logan's heart ached that the accident might have hurt the dog. If he lost Shadow… The survivor's guilt would crush him without his furry friend. Not to mention the loss of his new companion.

If it hadn't been for the distant car scaring their attacker off, Logan was one hundred percent sure the guy would have engaged and tried to finish the job of killing them.

Izzie sat at the farmhouse kitchen table after supper and buried her face in her hands, careful not to disturb the bandages Harper, one of the paramedics who met them at Stone Creek Ranch, had placed over her cuts. She'd let Lisa down, and she'd missed Whitney's disappearance. Where had she gone wrong? Was Will right? She thought her investigative skills ranked among the top. That was what her supervisor had told her on multiple occasions. But maybe the man had tried to be nice and lied.

"It's time for you to put the past behind you." Her mother's voice jerked her from her pity party.

"What do you mean?" She loved her mom and shared everything with her, except her past with Will.

Hannah Sinclair, not known for her subtly, slid a chair from the table and sat across from Izzie. "You are doing the best you can."

"But."

Her mom held up a hand. "I have ears. I've heard you kids talk. From what I understand, you and Daniel had nothing as far as evidence in Lisa's disappearance. That's not on you."

"It is though. I'm the sheriff. I should have searched harder. Thought of all the different possibilities."

"Oh really? Would you have found that body in the woods any faster? I don't think so."

"You don't understand. It's my job to know."

Her mom arched an eyebrow. "So I should have known your father was cheating on me years before I caught him, since I was his wife?"

Izzie jerked like her mom had slapped her. "No, Mom. The entire community had no idea."

"Well…"

"It's not the same."

"It isn't? Hindsight is a wonderful thing but doesn't help us in the present." Her mom's gaze latched on to her. "Or I should know what happened to my daughter in Dallas to make her doubt herself when she's the best sheriff Rollins has ever had?"

"What?" Izzie's heart pounded. How had her mom found out?

"Honey, I'm not clueless. You changed in Dallas. Something or someone made you question your worth. I have my suspicions, but I refuse to push." Her mom reached over and patted her hand. "Eventually, you'll tell me or someone you trust. I don't care which, as long as it helps you see what a wonderful woman and sheriff you are."

Izzie gaped at her mother. Had her fears and insecurities been that obvious?

"Search your heart, honey. Find that confidence again. I'm going to check on that sweet pup, Shadow." Hannah stood and pushed in her chair. "And maybe it's time for you to trust God with your fears." She left Izzie staring at the doorway.

Had she heard her mother mutter, "If I ever find that man, I'm going to give him a piece of my mind"?

Wow, so much for keeping secrets around that woman.

She sighed. Letting go of the pain and fears would be amazing. But it wasn't that easy. Will had done a number on her, and she continued to struggle to climb her way out of the lack-of-self-esteem cellar he'd thrown her into.

Gah! Izzie strode out the back door and to the horse barn. She couldn't tell her mom or Logan. Not yet. But Firefly would listen to her without judgment.

Shadow lay on the couch with his head on Logan's leg as Payton examined him. He dug his fingers into the dog's fur. The motion—comforting and instinctual even in the short time the pair had been together. The accident had twisted Logan's stomach in knots and confused him at the same time. Izzie had added bruises and cuts to her already battered body, and his shoulder and hip ached from the force of the collision. Who had run them off the road?

"Shadow's good to go. He might be stiff just like you will be from the jolt to your body, but I didn't find any injuries." Payton packed her vet bag. "And thank you for using a harness seat belt for him. It saved him from serious harm."

"Thanks for examining him. I appreciate it." His pulse raced. If he lost Shadow…

She waved him off. "No problem. I'm glad I could help. Now, if you'll excuse me, I have an early morning tomorrow."

Payton and her mom passed each other at the living room doorway. Miss Hannah hadn't changed, other than a few gray hairs. She'd become his second mom during his youth.

"There's that sweet boy." Hannah strode to Shadow's side and scratched his head. The dog rolled over, produced his belly and groaned. The woman laughed and obliged the dog. "You're quite the character."

"That he is." Logan smiled at the crazy canine. "I don't know what I'd do without him."

Hannah sat on the other end of the couch, continuing to pet Shadow. "I heard you had a rough time on your last mission."

His gaze flicked to her.

She chuckled. "Relax. No one told me details, but it doesn't take a genius to put the pieces together."

He had no idea how to respond. To do so meant acknowledging her suspicions.

"Shadow seems to be helping with your survivor's guilt."

His mouth fell open. "Wait. How?"

"Are you denying it?"

"Not when it's the truth. But I don't go around advertising it." He hated talking about it. And the looks of pity—no. Just no.

"I can understand that. When I discovered my husband's infidelity, I didn't want anyone to know. I was embarrassed. And mad. Boy, was I mad. I tried to save our marriage, but he had no intention of changing his lifestyle. That's when I kicked him out." She exhaled. "Then the guilt hit."

"I had no idea. I'm sorry you went through all that. But for the life of me, I can't figure out why you're telling me this."

"Because you need to hear it." A sad smile formed on her lips. "Depression hit hard. I struggled to keep going. The guilt of taking my children's father away from them and my own insecurity over not feeling like I was good enough to keep my husband happy almost took me under. But I had to keep going. I had kids to raise. You know what I figured out in those dark days?"

Logan shook his head.

"That I caused my own pain."

"How? *He* cheated on *you*."

"That he did, but it didn't change how I felt." She tilted her head. "Answer me this. Whatever happened on that mission, did you do your best with the information you had at the time?"

Had he? He thought for a moment, racking his brain. "Yes."

She reached across his dog and gripped his fingers. "I can't imagine what you went through. Nor can I completely understand PTSD. But I can tell you this. You have to forgive yourself. You just admitted you did your best. Now it's time to put it behind you. You'll never forget, but you can forgive yourself."

"It's not that easy, Miss Hannah."

The woman snorted. "I didn't say it was. I said it would be healing. It wasn't until I allowed myself grace that I started living again." She squeezed his fingers. "I'll let you and Shadow have a moment together. I'm sure you could use it after the events of the day."

She wasn't wrong. Logan required time to process what had occurred and a bit of quiet time with God. "Where's Izzie?"

"If I were to guess, she's out talking to Firefly."

Logan chuckled. "Did you do a hit-and-run with your wisdom on her like you did with me?"

"Maybe." She smirked. "I wish the circumstances were different, but I'm happy you're home, Logan. We've missed you."

"Thanks, Miss Hannah. For everything."

"If you'll excuse me, morning at the ranch comes early."

"Good night."

"You too, sweet boy." She kissed the top of his head and waltzed away.

His gaze lingered on the doorway where Hannah had disappeared. Her words rattled in his brain. Could he forgive himself for not saving Monty?

Shadow crawled into his lap and licked his cheek.

Logan wrapped his arms around the dog and buried his face in the canine's fur.

"I miss him, Shadow. He trusted me, and I let him down. How am I supposed to forgive myself for not saving him? And what am I supposed to do about Izzie?" Could he open up to her and put the past behind him?

SIX

Nightmares had filled Izzie's fitful sleep. Her mother's words had triggered memories she'd tried but failed to shove into the recesses of her mind. A yawn cracked her jaw. Coffee would be a necessity for work. With her department vehicle totaled and waiting on a new sheriff's SUV to arrive, Izzie and Logan caught a ride with Daniel and grabbed her personal vehicle from her house. The three of them, minus Shadow, who had stayed with her mom on the ranch, had moved to the sheriff's office after a quick stop at Saddle Sips for the much-needed caffeine.

She commandeered the conference room. The trio had made three lists on the whiteboard: possible victims, suspects and evidence. Izzie tapped her pen on her chin and stared at the victims list of four names. "Focus on Lisa and Whitney."

Daniel paused mid-bite of his pastry. "Why only them and not Carrie and Natalie too?"

"Because, dear brother, we know Whitney and Lisa. It'll be easier to compare their lives. If we find a commonality between them, we can cross-check with the other two women."

"Which, in turn, might narrow the investigation in the broader search." Logan nodded. "I like it."

For the next thirty minutes, they brainstormed who might have had the motive and opportunity to kidnap Lisa and Whitney, and listed the women's similarities.

"Well, that didn't help as much as I would have liked. Not

much more than we originally knew. Both are barrel racers around the same age, both have brown hair and brown eyes and both delivered messages when they left." She used air quotes around the word *left*. "Whitney had a boyfriend. Lisa dated but wasn't in a serious relationship."

"That about sums it up. I'll double-check Carrie's and Natalie's info, but I expect more of the same." The screech of Daniel's laptop sliding across the table pierced the air. "Oops. Sorry." The keyboard clicked as he dove into confirming their suspicions.

Izzie rubbed her forehead in hopes of chasing away the throbbing ache. The entire session had mimicked throwing darts at a target blindfolded. But at least the cold case had warmed up.

"Hold on you two. The coroner's report just landed in my inbox."

"Well?" Izzie tossed her pen on the table.

"Hold your horses, sis. I have to open the file. There. Let me see." His eyes shifted back and forth. "In a nutshell, Carrie sustained injuries prior to her death. Cause of death was starvation over time. He made a note that he believes she was given food and water to prolong her life for a couple of months, but minimal, and eventually starved to death."

Logan shook his head. "That's torture."

"Exactly what the coroner stated."

"If he has Lisa." Logan's gut-wrenching tone broke Izzie's heart.

"Don't. You'll only torment yourself." She couldn't allow him to suffer in the what-ifs. "Anything else pertinent?"

"The animals had done a number on her, but the coroner was able to detect markings around one ankle like she'd been shackled and fought against the restraint. The coroner also timed her death to several days before you discovered her body."

"So, she goes missing around eight months ago then Lisa two months ago. It's like our abductor is finding replacements." Logan closed his eyes and exhaled.

"That's how it appears. Assuming we haven't gone completely off the rails on our deduction."

The room grew quiet. Each of them deep in thought.

Izzie grabbed her pen from where she'd tossed it on the table. "Since Lisa lives here, I'd like to start by talking to Keats about men connected to the rodeo. Then check into the guys she dated or had contact with."

Logan pointed at the whiteboard next to Harvey Powers's name. "That loner Powers is creeping to the top for me."

"Why him?" Daniel asked without looking up from his laptop.

"The fact he lost his wife and daughter and turned into a recluse after their deaths, coupled with his work-from-home job. It makes me wonder." Logan lowered his hand then looked down—almost as if he went to pet Shadow and realized the dog wasn't there. It had to be tough on him to spend the day without his companion.

"I'll add him to my list and speak with him on my way to the rodeo grounds." Izzie typed notes into her phone and updated the working list.

"I'll go with you and leave Daniel to his digging." Logan crossed his arms over his chest.

Izzie shook her head. "I prefer if you stay and create a detailed timeline."

Logan pinched his lips together. "What about the guy after you?"

"Logan. I'm the sheriff. I won't be stupid, but I can't stop working." She refused to have the city council question her abilities.

"Fine. I'll work on the timeline," Logan grumbled. "But I don't like you going alone."

Yeah, she didn't either, but she wouldn't allow the maniac who had attacked her to dictate her job. She considered it for a moment. "I'd say yes, but we need that sequence of events as soon as possible. Lisa is running out of time."

Logan stared at her and voiced the words he'd wondered from the beginning. "You really think she's still alive?"

"I have to. The alternative is unacceptable."

He inhaled and nodded. "Then I'll get busy." He drew several straight lines on the board then picked up the papers they'd filled with notes and flipped through them.

Izzie called the Rodeo Director and arranged a meeting. "I'm heading over to Saddle Sips to speak with Powers then to the rodeo grounds for my meeting with Keats. Let me know if you two come up with anything."

"Will do, sis." Daniel waved, but his eyes stayed glued to the computer.

"Be safe, Izzie." The concern in Logan's tone almost made her turn around—almost.

Izzie left the guys with their assignments and strode to the main office. "Hey, Cory. I'll be at the rodeo grounds with Mr. Keats if you need me."

"Thanks, Sheriff."

She exited the station and headed to Saddle Sips to chat with Harvey Powers since he spent most of his time there. After discovering the man hadn't made an appearance at the coffee shop, she continued to the rodeo grounds.

Donovan's office was located off the arena, so she parked near the horse barn that sat adjacent to the main offices. With time to spare before her appointment, she dropped her booted foot from her SUV and snicked the door closed. Dust kicked up around each step as she made her way inside.

Stalls lined the extra-wide aisle. The scent of hay and manure hung heavy in the air. Footlockers, filled with brushes, hoof picks and other personal supplies, sat in the middle of the walkway. A few lawn chairs dotted the belongings—the fabric coated with stray horsehair and hay dust. The barn was extra quiet today, except for the occasional soft nicker or the shuffle of hooves against the dirt. Most of the rodeo community had gone to compete a few counties over.

For years, Donovan allowed those on the circuit or those who had competed in the past to use the Marshall County grounds to board their horses. The never-empty barn teemed with activity year-round.

Izzie approached the first enclosure. "Hi there, Rocky. How's it going?" She ran a hand over the horse's nose. She'd known Rocky's owner, Jeb, for a long time. The man no longer rode broncs but continued to be a staple around the rodeos, dispensing wisdom. The horse bobbed his head up and down. "Sorry, no treat this morning."

She moved to the next stalls, greeting the animals who'd stayed home from the rodeo, until she came to Zeus. The bad-tempered horse had a reputation around the county. "Hey, Zeus. You still hate everyone?" The animal snorted and scraped his hoof on the ground, kicking up small clumps of dirt and straw. Izzie waved a hand in front of her face, chasing away the dust particles floating in the air. "Yup. Still the same grumpy old man. I don't know how Chet puts up with you." Chet had a way with Zeus, but anyone else, that horse would buck off in two seconds flat. She wondered what had happened to the black quarter horse to make him the way he was. And there went her soft side, which Will had complained made her a liability in the law enforcement profession. Always trying to figure out the reason behind someone's—or in this case a horse's—actions. Izzie thought it helped her be a better sheriff, but Will's words continued to bog her down.

Izzie mentally chased away her wandering thoughts and let the comfort of the familiar horses and barn sink in. The only thing missing—the loud ruckus of voices that accompanied the group of competitors and friends. She smiled, remembering the time she'd spent barrel racing.

The sensation of icy fingers crawled up her neck. She spun,

jerking her gaze from one side of the barn to the other. Either someone was watching her, or paranoia had sunk in its claws.

Her phone buzzed in her pocket. She jolted. Her heart raced faster than a horse spooked by a rattlesnake. *It's only your phone, Izzie.* She steadied her galloping pulse and ran her gaze across the barn again. She withdrew her phone and answered without taking her eyes off her surroundings. "Sheriff Sinclair."

"Izzie?"

"Hey, Daniel. What's up?"

"Logan's here and you're on speaker. First, are you okay?"

Leave it to her brother to be in tune with her. "I'm good. Just talking with my horse friends."

"You're already at the rodeo grounds?" Logan asked.

"Harvey didn't show at the coffee shop today, so I came on out for a little me time."

"Face it. You're as bad as Grace."

Izzie smiled at the mention of her brother Cooper's new wife and the woman's love for horses. "It's a girl thing."

Daniel laughed. "As if. We guys take our horses seriously too."

"I can't argue with that. I know you didn't call to talk about equine therapy. What have you got for me?"

She heard car doors close and an engine start.

"We're coming your way. I want to hear your conversation with Keats," Logan said.

"I'm fine with that. Now, tell me what you found." She studied the dark corners of the barn but found nothing amiss.

"I started the missing person's search throughout Texas and moved outward from there to the surrounding states. You're not going to like it," Daniel said.

"It doesn't matter if I like it or not. Just tell me."

Daniel's words yanked her from her musing. "I discovered a total of eight barrel racers from Texas and nearby states that have gone missing six months apart over a four-year period."

Izzie froze. "Eight women?"

"Lisa would be number nine." She hadn't missed the worry in Logan's tone.

"Have any of their bodies been found other than Carrie's?"

"Yes." Daniel's soft answer tore at her heart.

She hated that the loss of life might lead them to her friend, but she'd take anything right now. She had to find Lisa before it was too late. "Contact the departments involved and request the files."

"Already done. Cory will call when the information arrives."

Izzie trusted her administrative assistant with the task. The woman was a lifesaver with scheduling and organization. "I'm sure she'll hound the offices involved if they aren't moving fast enough."

Daniel laughed. "No doubt."

"I'm really hoping someone didn't abduct all these women." Logan brought the conversation back to the seriousness of the topic.

"Looking at the files and determining that will be the first order of business once we get the info."

Zeus's eyes widened, and he stomped on the ground, huffing.

"What's wrong, buddy?"

"Who are you talking to?" Logan asked.

"Zeus."

"That animal is scary." Daniel made a fake shiver sound.

"Says the man who jumps in the arena with two-thousand-pound bulls."

"He's really upset."

She stiffened at Daniel's observation.

"Izzie. I don't like it. Get out of there," Logan commanded.

She caught a flicker of movement from the corner of her eye. Before she could react, a forceful shove sent her stumbling forward. Her phone slipped from her grasp and clattered to the ground. She struck the stall door hard, her arms absorbing the impact as she hit the metal bars. Her knee smacked the wood panel at the bottom, sending a zing through her leg. A strong arm snaked around her neck. She thrashed and clawed, desperate to break free from the man's grasp as he opened Zeus's gate.

"Izzie!" Logan's voice rose from the fallen phone.

The man's grip tightened, cutting off her airway, rendering her unable to call out for help. The blessed sound of a distant siren floated on the air. With a brutal shove, the attacker pushed her into the Zeus's stall. Izzie's head spun from the lack of oxygen. She struggled to regain her footing, sucking in shallow breaths. Zeus's nostrils flared, and he stamped his hooves, swinging his head with a force that clipped Izzie. Knocked off balance, she stumbled backward. Her skull struck the hard metal gate of the stall. A swarm of black dots swirled in her vision. She crumpled to the ground and curled into a tight ball.

"Help me, Logan." She prayed he'd heard her plea, but she wasn't sure she'd spoken the words aloud.

"Step on it, Daniel." Logan snatched the phone from the dashboard and pressed it against his ear, trying to hear over the wailing siren that Daniel activated. The scuffle and lack of response from Izzie had Logan's heart pounding against his rib cage. Regret gnawed at him. He should have stayed with her instead of working at the office with Daniel. The thought of losing Izzie threatened to unravel the last threads of his sanity. He yearned for the calming presence of Shadow. The dog's comfort had pulled him through dark days. But he'd left the animal at the ranch with Miss Hannah. Shadow deserved the love and pampering Izzie's mom would provide after the accident. But that didn't take away his need for the dog's presence.

"She's strong. She'll be okay."

Logan's eyes snapped to Daniel. "Are you saying that to calm me down or yourself?" Desperation crept into his voice.

The man shrugged. "Both." Daniel's white-knuckled grip on the steering wheel belied his easygoing tone.

Logan had to stuff his emotions aside. Find the Teamguy inside. The one that analyzed, planned and acted. Not the current emotional mess.

Daniel took a hard right into the parking lot. Logan grabbed the handle next to the door and held on. The truck fishtailed and skidded to a stop in front of the barn.

Logan's boots hit the ground before Daniel slammed the vehicle into Park. He sprinted into the building. "Izzie!" He targeted in on the agitated horse toward the end of the aisle. "Izzie!"

"Here." Her quiet words wove through the animal's snorting and high-pitched neigh.

"I'm coming. Hold on." He slid to a halt and examined the sight in front of him. Izzie huddled in the corner of the stall by the gate while the horse pawed at the ground near her. It wouldn't surprise him if she had scrape marks on her legs from the horse's hooves.

Daniel rushed in.

Logan held up a fist, slowing the man as to not scare the horse more. "Move over here—slowly. Open the gate while I pull her out. Then shut the thing so that crazy animal doesn't escape."

"You got it." Daniel eased toward him. "Ready?"

"Go."

Daniel yanked the gate open several feet, and Logan grabbed the back of Izzie's shirt and dragged her to safety. As soon as Izzie's boots cleared the entrance, Daniel slammed the gate shut and latched it. The man drew his weapon and began clearing the barn.

Between the accident the previous day and pulling Izzie from the crazed horse, Logan's healing shoulder burned. He pushed aside the discomfort and knelt beside her. "Do you need an ambulance?"

She shook her head and winced. "Give me a second."

Logan brushed the hair from her face and tucked it behind her ear.

"Is everything okay in here? I saw you boys hightailing it from the parking lot." Donovan Keats came to an abrupt stop when he spotted Izzie lying on the ground. "Izzie? What happened?"

Izzie struggled to sit up.

Logan supported her back and gave her his hand to help her. "I'd like to hear that answer as well."

She scooted to rest her back on a bale of hay in the middle of the aisle. Dust and straw covered her clothes and hair.

Daniel jogged back in. "The guy's gone." He scooped Izzie's cell phone off the ground and handed it to her.

"Thanks." Her hands trembled as she accepted her phone. "I got here early for our appointment and came to visit with the horses. While I was on the phone with these guys—" she motioned toward him and Daniel "—someone attacked me from behind and threw me in with Zeus. Let's just say that horse wasn't fond of my presence in the stall with him." She lifted her arm and looked at it.

Red scratches marred her skin along with the black-and-blue marks that had begun to appear.

Logan's heart kicked up a notch. "Did Zeus get your head?"

"No. But I'm guessing I have similar markings on my leg."

"You need to get that cleaned up." Daniel pointed to her arm. "With all the manure and dirt, I don't want those scrapes getting infected."

Keats folded his arms across his chest. "I agree with your brother."

"I promise to shower once I'm back at the ranch. Until then, I'll go wash my arm and face in the bathroom." Logan helped her stand, and she gestured to the shower room at the end of the building. "If y'all will excuse me."

His eyes never left her as she limped to the bathroom. "Looks like Zeus got her leg pretty good."

"Just don't say anything. That woman will lay you out flat if you suggest she's hurt." Daniel rubbed the back of his neck. "Don't know what that's all about, but she's touchy when it comes to stuff like that."

"That girl thinks she has something to prove. I wish she'd realize that she's an excellent sheriff." Keats sounded more like a concerned father than a rodeo director.

"Do you know why?" Logan prayed the man had the answer to the question that had plagued him.

"Not a clue."

Logan shifted his gaze to Daniel. "What about you?"

"Nope. All I know is when she came back from Dallas, her self-confidence had taken a nosedive. She's never talked about it."

The conversation ceased when Izzie exited the bathroom and strode toward them. Her limp seemed more pronounced with each step.

"Was your leg scraped too?" After what the guys said, Logan hoped he hadn't overstepped.

"Just bruised. My jeans protected my skin." Her gaze shifted to each of them. "Now that my up-close-and-personal experience with Zeus is over, I'd like to go ahead with our meeting, Mr. Keats."

"Certainly. How about we talk here instead of walking all the way to my office?"

Izzie smirked. "I know what you're doing, and I appreciate it." Her gaze traveled the inside of the barn. "But let's take this outside."

Logan followed her gaze and scanned the interior. Was the person who threw her in the stall with Zeus here—watching, listening? He didn't think so since Daniel had cleared the barn.

The group headed to the parking lot.

"What exactly happened in there?" Keats asked.

Izzie explained how the man attacked her. "If it hadn't been for Daniel hitting the siren, I think he would have strangled me to death. And you know how long that takes. It's not a quick process. When we heard the siren, he chose to throw me in with Zeus and get out of there. I'm assuming he hoped the animal would stomp me to death."

"I'm glad we came to meet up with you. If not..." Daniel let the thought trail off.

Logan opened the driver's door of Daniel's truck. "Why don't you have a seat while we talk." Without complaint, she crawled in, hung her legs over the side and slouched against the seat. The woman looked done in.

For the next twenty minutes, they discussed everyone from the bronc rider Isaac Sample to his board members. Keats had great insight into the people around him, but nothing that pointed them to a killer.

Once they'd finished the interview and Keats promised to email her information on the men who worked on or around the rodeo, he and Daniel chatted away in front of him and Izzie.

Logan leaned in. "I think it's time we add your name to the list of victims. This guy might not want to kidnap you, but he definitely wants you out of the picture."

She released a long stream of air. "I hate to admit it, but you're right."

"And plan on having a personal bodyguard."

Izzie bristled. "I—"

He held up his hand, stopping her lecture. "It's not about ability. It's about someone having your six and allowing you to do your job without looking over your shoulder." And about his need to protect her, but he refused to mention that. If she had any inkling as to his real motive, she'd walk away from him—again. He didn't know if his heart could take the rejection a second time.

SEVEN

Logan sat in the Stone Creek Ranch living room and rolled his neck side to side. The muscles had tightened the moment Izzie's attacker had ambushed her in the rodeo barn. Being helpless brought back a ton of memories. And not good ones. His mind turned to his twin sister. He'd come to find Lisa and life had thrown obstacles in his path. Guilt gnawed at him for losing focus. But how could he not be there for Izzie?

Shadow whined at his feet.

"Come on up, boy. Miss Hannah said you've been snuggling on the couch most of the day." He patted the cushion next to him.

Shadow hopped up and nuzzled his neck. Logan wrapped his arms around the animal and closed his eyes. The scent of sugar cookies tickled his nose. Miss Hannah had bathed and brushed Shadow until his black coat gleamed. He'd thank her later, but for now he'd soak in the comfort of his furry friend.

Today was a testament to how essential the dog's support was to Logan's emotional well-being. He'd reached for Shadow multiple times to calm himself but had come up empty. His commander had been right—like always—to insist Logan accept the service dog. He'd have to remember to thank the man once he found Lisa.

Several minutes later, he released his hold. "Thanks, buddy."

The dog licked his cheek then awkwardly circled on unsteady paws and plopped down, resting his head in Logan's lap.

"Find a cozy spot?" He smoothed a hand down the dog's back.

His furry friend huffed.

"I hear ya. It's been a long couple of days." The dog's presence once again settled his runaway what-if thoughts.

"Have space on that couch for me?" Izzie limped into the room.

"Sure." Logan gestured to the other side. "Shadow's a bit of a bed hog. Couch hog in this situation. But he'll share."

She scooted Shadow's backside over a little to give herself a place to sit. The dog glanced back and gave Izzie a *what are you doing?* look then laid his head back in Logan's lap.

"How's the leg?"

"Sore." She touched the side of her thigh and snorted. "Good thing I like the color purple."

Logan never should've stayed with Daniel. He could have prevented her pain if only he'd gone with her. "I'm just happy you weren't hurt worse."

Her hand went to her neck. Two layers of bruises stood out. Dark purple peeked out underneath the red from earlier that day. "Can't say I want to repeat that."

"Yo, why wasn't I invited to the party?" Daniel sauntered in and dropped onto the recliner.

Izzie rolled her eyes. "Since we didn't have the opportunity to discuss your findings, tell me what you know about those missing girls."

"I don't have the full files yet but do have the summarized reports."

"Well, don't keep us in suspense." Izzie motioned with her hand for him to keep going.

"As you know, there are eight. Nine if we include Lisa. Each taken approximately six months apart, according to the estimated dates."

"All barrel racers?" Logan asked.

"Yes. I should receive the full files tomorrow. From what I have, one thing that stands out is that all the women are around twenty-five to thirty, give or take a year or two. All barrel racers, and they all have brown hair and brown eyes."

"So if the same guy abducted each of them, he has a type." Logan's dinner stirred in his belly. He hated the thought of his sister being in the hands of a possible serial killer.

"Exactly. Young women. Brunette. Barrel racers."

"Like Lisa." Izzie closed her eyes and dropped her chin to her chest.

"We have to find her." He resisted the urge to bolt and run full tilt into town—shake everyone who'd seen her in the days prior to her disappearance for more information. He inhaled, settling his desperation to act. The SEALs had taught him discipline. To strategize. To come up with backup plans for his backups. But with his sister involved and Izzie's life threatened, his training jumped out of the plane and free-fell to the earth. He prayed the parachute would open before he hit the ground and his training would overtake his panic. Shadow pawed at his chest. Logan blinked and ran his hand down the dog's back. Three deep breaths later, he met Daniel's gaze. "What else do you have?"

Daniel shrugged. "Not much."

"We have three different areas in three different states. With that new information, and assuming it's the same man, he has to have a job that allows him to travel without calling attention to himself." Izzie shifted to sheriff mode. "Who do we have on the suspect list who fits that?"

"You know it might not be one of them?"

Izzie leveled Daniel with a glare that would send most grown men screaming in the other direction. "Trust me. I know I didn't do enough, and the case went cold. But this is where we are."

Daniel held his hand up. "I didn't mean anything by it. Just that we shouldn't limit our scope."

Logan's gaze drifted from Izzie to Daniel and back. His friend had stepped in the muck.

"Fine." With downcast eyes, Izzie fiddled with her phone. What had happened to her? "I agree. But let's focus on what we have."

Logan could get behind data, and at the same time support Izzie. "The guy has to be able to leave for extended periods of time, or he's lived in, worked in or visited all three locations over the past four years. I agree with Izzie, let's start with the people we know and move out from there."

The gratitude in her gaze made his heart ache. He wanted to pummel whoever had stolen her self-confidence. "What about Harvey Powers? You said he lost his wife and child a few years back."

Izzie nodded. "He's a loner and works remote. He could leave town for weeks at a time and no one would be the wiser."

"What's his history beyond that?" Logan asked.

"He grew up around here." Daniel rubbed his chin with his finger and thumb. "I think he steer wrestled back in the day. He's forty-two. A bit before our time. He's a rodeo volunteer so he'd be aware of who the barrel racers are and have access to the women."

"He's a definite possibility." Logan buried his fingers in Shadow's fur.

Izzie scowled. "He seems a bit on the older side, but he's in good shape and around the right height of the man who attacked me."

"We'll keep him on the list since he's still in the rodeo community. Then there's Grey Chapman. He's thirty-four and a pharmaceutical sales rep when he's not working on the rodeo board. He moved here from Oklahoma two years ago." Daniel scanned his notes. "He matches the region in Oklahoma of victims one and two, and of course Carrie, Natalie, Whitney and Lisa here in Texas. But he never lived in Arkansas. At least as far as I can tell."

Izzie scrunched her forehead. "He has a job that allows him to travel, so maybe he's been to Arkansas. I'm not willing to cross him off the list."

"I'm with Izzie." Logan's pulse increased. The more they talked the more frustrated he became. He tamped down his nervous energy. *Come on, you're a SEAL. Man up.*

Logan shifted on the couch. Shadow grumbled and rolled onto his back. Logan obliged and scratched the dog's tummy. "What about those guys she met at the feedstore?"

"Ah, yes. The ever-smarmy sales rep, Peter Walace, who thinks he's God's gift to women." Daniel fake shivered. "By the way, he's not."

"Does he have a type?" Why had his sister dated him?

"Let's see." Daniel tapped his chin. "Female. That's his type."

Izzie chuckled. "True."

"So why did Lisa date him if he's that much of a player?"

"I don't consider one cup of coffee *dating*." Izzie used air quotes around the word. "It was probably self-preservation. Accept his offer to go for coffee so he'd back off."

Logan bobbed his head up and down in silent understanding. "Wasn't there another guy?"

"Raymond Burke. Lisa met him at Saddle Sips several times. Seems to be a nice guy. He's a graphic designer. We had him update the sheriff's department website not long ago. From what he told me, he came to Rollins to take care of Hudson Ingall's father. Apparently, Raymond and Hudson became friends working construction in Houston. Hudson died in a work accident years ago. Raymond promised to help if Hudson's dad ever needed him. When the older man passed away, Raymond stayed. I think he lives over on Cedar Street."

"Obviously he's not working construction anymore. Did he live anywhere other than Houston?"

"I'm not one-hundred-percent, but I don't think he left that area until he moved here. But I could be wrong. I wasn't really looking at his address history when we hired him for the website." Izzie's shoulders drooped.

"His remote job makes him stand out. But the other information we have about his previous location doesn't fit our parameters."

The dark circles under Izzie's eyes concerned Logan. So far, they hadn't made much progress, and Izzie's energy had waned. "I think we should take a break and look at it fresh tomorrow once we have the complete files and are back in the office."

Izzie stiffened. "Another hour won't hurt us. I say we keep going."

"Izzie. You're exhausted. I'm as driven to find Lisa as you are, but we won't be any good to her if we don't rest and recharge."

"Fine." Izzie pushed from the couch and limped out of the living room.

Logan watched her leave then shifted to look at Daniel. "What just happened?"

Daniel laughed. "You, my friend, should be amazed that your head is still attached to your body. By the way, I've spread the word to the ranch hands. They'll keep an eye out for trouble." Daniel rose and waved. "I know I can use some sleep. I'll catch you later."

Logan remained seated and searched his brain for what had set Izzie off while he loved on Shadow.

Hannah Sinclair waltzed into the room and sat in the recliner Daniel had abandoned. "I saw Izzie hightail it toward the barn. Want to tell me why my little girl is seeking refuge with the horses?" The woman's tone didn't hold judgment or anger, just simple concern.

He told her about the exchange, and his recommendation. "Apparently, my suggestion hit a nerve."

"Oh, son. I promise, you did nothing wrong. She's struggled since moving home to Rollins. She refuses to talk about the why. But I have that mom intuition that it has to do with a man."

Logan's heart rate spiked. "He didn't… She's…"

"Relax, Logan. My mother instincts say that no one hurt her—at least not physically."

"I want her to talk to me, but she shuts down anytime we edge toward that conversation."

Hannah jutted her chin toward Shadow. "You have your own struggles. I'm guessing she might finally expose her problems if you'd open up to her. Allow her to see it's okay to be vulnerable."

His jaw dropped. Hannah wanted him to spill his guts?

The older woman chuckled. "She needs to trust she can expose her fears without judgment. I can't be that for her. I'm her mom. She knows I'll always be her number one fan." Hannah rose and patted him on the shoulder as she walked by. "Think about it."

His heart pounded against his ribs. Could he do it? Could he rip the scab off the emotional wounds and expose the entire story behind the guilt that wouldn't let go?

Izzie leaned against the stall door, running her hand down Firefly's nose. The comforting scent of hay and horses filled the quiet barn. She'd snuck out to the barn after Logan's suggestion had stepped on her confidence. He hadn't meant anything by it. She knew that. But the self-doubt had struck hard. She exhaled. The weight of the past couple of days pressed down on her. The sensation of danger not far from her thoughts. Horses shifted in their stalls. Her constant anchor during the storms in her life.

"Firefly, if I don't figure this out, I'll lose my best friend." If she hadn't already. She nuzzled the horse's neck. Tears pricked her eyes. "And then there's Logan. What do I do about him?"

She swallowed the boulder-size lump in her throat. The man's steady presence calmed her. She should have said yes to his invitation for a date all those years ago. But dear ol' Daddy's betrayal had lingered. And what had she done a few years later? Gone into the arms of a man who belittled her.

"I don't make the best decisions." She peered into Firefly's black eyes. It was like the animal understood her plight and empathized with her. "What am I going to do?" And here she stood again, pouring her heart out to a four-legged creature and not God. She really had to work on that.

The barn door creaked.

She whipped her Glock from its holster and aimed at the sound.

"Whoa. It's just me." Logan held up his hands in surrender.

She closed her eyes and lowered her weapon. "Sorry."

"No need to apologize. I'm glad to see you're taking the threat against you seriously." He stepped inside and closed the door behind him. She hadn't missed that he'd double-checked the latch.

Shadow padded beside him. His black eyes scanned the room before settling on Izzie. The dog's head tilted one way and then the other.

"Your mom said I'd find you here." Logan took a few steps closer, stopping at the stall next to Firefly's. "Needed some air?"

Izzie shrugged, forcing a small smile. "Something like that."

He opened his mouth then closed it. No doubt stopping himself from scolding her.

Well, she was the sheriff for the love of everything. She could take care of herself. Yeah, right. She'd done a bang-up job of that and had the bruises to prove it. Izzie sighed and gestured toward the horse in the stall beside Logan. "That's Lisa's horse, Cricket."

Logan turned and made a clicking sound with his tongue. Cricket lifted his head and ambled to the gate. Logan patted the horse's cheek. "Hey there, buddy. Long time no see."

For a long moment, they stood in companionable silence. Logan traced the white streak that ran the length of Cricket's forehead to the end of his nose.

He scanned the interior of the barn with a trained eye before releasing a long, slow breath. "I've spent years fighting battles overseas. The things I've seen, the people I couldn't save..." His Adam's apple bobbed. "They don't just fade. Some nights, they refuse to stay silent. The memories taunt me. Telling me I should've done more. I should've been better." He ran a hand through his hair. Shadow plastered himself to Logan's side. His fingers immediately went to the dog's head.

Izzie's chest tightened. "Logan—"

He held up a hand, stopping her from responding. "You know what happened on my last mission. Shadow is a byproduct of the aftermath. Yes, I have PTSD from it, and my time as a SEAL in general. I've come to grips with that. I'm learning how to counter the flashbacks. But it's the survivor's guilt that cripples me. Why wasn't it me who died?" He sucked in an audible breath. "I live in the land of what-ifs. What if it had taken us ten minutes longer to get to the village? What if I'd had time to disarm the device? What if I'd made the call to leave a minute earlier?"

"That's a lot of guilt to hold on to." She'd known that Logan had suffered both physically and mentally but hadn't realized the true reason. To survive when your brother-in-arms next you to hadn't... She blinked back tears.

"It is. I know it in here." He tapped his head. "But my heart... I'm having issues letting it go."

Silence stretched between them. Unsure what to say, she

reached out. Her fingers brushed against his. He flipped his hand and clasped hers in a gentle hold.

"I'm sorry you had to go through that."

"I don't need your sympathy. But I could use your support."

"You've got it." She nibbled on her lower lip. Should she confess her fears? His willingness to be vulnerable had whittled away at the cage around her heart.

"Come on. Let's sit. Both of us are sore from everything that's happened." Logan led her to a row of hay bales.

Once seated, Shadow impersonated a lapdog and crawled up and sprawled across their thighs.

She laughed. "He doesn't know his size, does he?" Izzie's fingers on her free hand absently stroked the dog's fur. "Do you ever feel like no matter how hard you try, it's never enough?"

Logan's expression softened. "Yeah. More times than I can count."

She swallowed, gathering the courage to voice what she had buried for so long. "Back when I was in the academy, I thought I had everything figured out. I had a plan—a goal for the future. And then he came along."

"Who?"

She let out a humorless laugh. "Deputy Chief of the Criminal Investigations Group, Will Adler. My boyfriend—until he wasn't. I didn't work directly for him, but in the hierarchy of positions, he ranked as a superior officer. At first, he acted like he believed in me, but in the end, he berated me. Said I wasn't tough enough—not smart enough—for a career in law enforcement. His gaslighting was so complete that I started to believe it. Then he complained I had a heart of ice, and that I lacked in the role of a girlfriend as well. That's when I broke things off with him, but the humiliation didn't stop there. A couple of months later, he married someone else. Come to find out he wanted a trophy wife on his arm to help him climb the ranks. I had no desire to be that woman. According to what he told everyone, Janice fit the mold of what a law enforcement wife should be. Another dig to humiliate me."

Logan squeezed her hand, but didn't interrupt. He just listened.

"The sad part was I believed him. That I'd never measure up. That I wasn't girlfriend or wife material. That's when I knew I had to leave Dallas." She blinked back the sting in her eyes. "It's hard to trust my judgment after something like that. Hard to let anyone close again."

Logan looked at her. Understanding glistened in his eyes. "Maybe we're both scared to look beyond the past."

A sad smile tugged at her lips. "Probably."

Neither of them spoke, but something had shifted. A thread of understanding weaved between them. The past had shaped them, but maybe, just maybe, it didn't have to define them.

"Thank you for sharing. So many things make sense now."

"Back at ya." She stared at their joined hands. "What does this mean for us?"

Logan shrugged. "I hope we can see where this might go."

"I think I'd like that."

"Maybe once we find Lisa, I'll try asking you out again. Assuming that's okay with you."

Dating Logan terrified her and excited her at the same time. "More than."

"Not to break the moment or step on your independence, but you do know that you have self-appointed guardians watching out for you, right?"

She sighed. "I noticed. Garrett, our ranch hand, isn't as stealthy as he thinks he is. After what's happened over the past couple of days, I won't let my insecurities interfere with my safety."

"You're a capable sheriff. Don't let Will's manipulation cause you to doubt that."

"I'll try."

"Good." Logan's smile made her belly flutter like a thousand butterflies taking flight.

No matter what he thought, the man exuded confidence and compassion. Something she could learn from. And that she appreciated with the attempts on her life.

Now to set aside her fear of failing as a sheriff and find Lisa. Assuming Izzie's attacker didn't succeed, and she lived long enough to solve the case.

EIGHT

Logan had to give his navy therapist and Miss Hannah credit. After confessing his survivor's guilt to Izzie last night, he'd slept better than he had in a long time. Or maybe it had been the deeper connection that he and Izzie had forged. Whatever the case, he'd take it. Now, if only they could find his twin sister. One piece missing from his life.

He entered the kitchen and came to an abrupt halt in the doorway. Chaos was the best description he could come up with. Hannah talked on one phone, and Izzie paced while on another. Both animated in their conversations. Their voices a touch on the harried side. He eyed the half-full coffeepot, eased into the room with Shadow at his side and poured himself a cup of the bold brew. He leaned against the counter and sipped his coffee, waiting for either woman to finish and fill him in. Shadow lay next to him on the tile floor.

Izzie ended her call and released a heavy sigh.

Mug to his lips, he raised an eyebrow. "What's up?"

"The guys are in the back pasture. A coyote attacked one of the calves. She's alive but badly hurt. Garrett and Daniel took our new ranch hand, Steve, to check out the situation and bring the other cattle closer. We haven't had a problem with coyotes in a long time."

"Have they called Payton?"

Izzie nodded. "She's on her way."

He narrowed his gaze. "But that's not all, is it?"

"Unfortunately, no. Our neighbor spotted a hole in the fence out on the east pasture."

"And that's where they're bringing the cattle."

"Yup. I'm the only one available to go fix it before they push the cattle there."

"Then let's go." He refused to allow Izzie out of his sight. He hadn't been kidding last night about her self-appointed guardians. In one swig, he downed his cooled coffee and placed the cup in the sink.

She brushed her hand against his. Her gaze flicked to her mom. "I'm sorry we can't get to the office."

"The repair shouldn't take us long. Then we can jump back into the investigation. As much as I want Lisa to be our sole focus, I can't expect the world to stop. We take care of the immediate need then we can turn our full attention to the case."

"How can you be so calm?"

"I trust God will do His thing." Logan rubbed his chest. "It hurts to think that might not be getting my sister back. But if the worst happens, I know my sister will be with Him for eternity."

Tears pooled on Izzie's lashes. "I'm not sure I could be so accepting if it were one of my siblings."

"You do what you have to do. And I'm placing my trust in God." He held her shoulders and dipped his head to look in her eyes. "Now, what do you say we get that fence fixed so we can find Lisa. I might be waxing philosophically, but I'm anxious to take a look at those files coming in this morning."

She laughed. "Grab your boots. I'm calling the office." Izzie placed the call. "Hey, Cory. I'll be running late. Long story but there's a hole in the fence out in the east pasture, and I pulled the short straw… Yeah, well, you tell Daniel that… Have you received those files? Great. We'll be in as soon as we finish." Izzie hung up and turned to face him. "Let's go."

After grabbing tools and saddling the horses, Logan sat atop

Cricket. He patted the horse's neck. "I know you miss her. So do I." He hoped and prayed they found Lisa alive.

Izzie and Firefly eased next to him. "Ready?"

"Let's do this."

They took the horses out at a canter. Neither one of them wanted to waste more time. Shadow ran beside them, his pink tongue hanging out. The dog had recovered from the accident and appeared pleased to be out running through the grass. *Mental note to self. Buy a house with a big yard.* Logan smiled. That was the first time his mind allowed him to think beyond the here and now to the future.

When they approached the gap in the fence, Izzie dismounted and dropped the reins. The well-trained horse didn't move from his spot.

Logan rested his forearm on the saddle horn. "Well?"

"It wasn't deliberate if that's what you're asking." Izzie slipped on her leather gloves.

It *had* crossed his mind. "So, what happened?" He dropped to the ground and strode toward her without letting go of Cricket.

"You can release his reins. He won't go anywhere."

He glanced at the horse. "Are you sure?" The last thing he wanted was to lose Lisa's baby.

"Positive."

Logan hesitated but dropped the reins. Cricket lowered his head and munched on the grass like he couldn't care less if Logan was there or not.

"What caused the hole?" His gaze roamed the trees near the fence line. Had the attacker caused the chaos on purpose?

Izzie picked a piece of fur from the barbs. "It looks like a deer forced its way through. I'm guessing the poor thing is regretting its decision." She pointed at the dried blood.

"Ouch. What can I do to help?"

"Grab the wire in the leather pouch."

With another scan of the area, he pulled out a small loop of wire and handed it to her. It might have been a deer, but Logan's suspicious nature had him on edge.

"I'm only doing a temporary job. Garrett can do the permanent fix later." Izzie patched the hole like a pro.

He held the old wire and handed her tools as she needed them. Shadow took that time to frolic like a pup in the field. Chasing butterflies in the wildflowers and pouncing at nothing in particular. Logan smiled at his antics. Yup, a big yard was on his list.

Izzie stepped back and brushed her gloved hands together. "There. That should hold for a while."

Logan moved to gather the reins of both horses.

She bent over to grab her tools.

A sharp crack filled the air. The horses reared and yanked against his hold. The force came close to dislocating his good shoulder. Logan recognized that sound. He held on to the leather straps and dropped to his knees behind the horses. His gaze jerked to the far end of the pasture, searching for the shooter. "Izzie?"

No answer.

He spun and found Izzie lying face down on the ground. His heart plummeted. "Izzie!"

Izzie's breaths came in pants. Another shot whizzed over her head. The bullet hit the ground inches from her head, spraying dirt. She had to move—had to get out of the shooter's line of sight. But her arms and legs had turned to mush.

"Izzie!"

She rolled her head, unwilling to lift it and create a target. "I'm good. I think."

"We need to take cover." He pointed to a copse of trees. "Can you move?"

"Maybe." She had no idea if her limbs would work.

"I'll come get you."

"No. Stay."

Concern lined his features. "On three."

She nodded and sucked in a deep breath.

"One, two, three!"

Izzie pushed to her hands and feet and bear crawled to the trees. Another shot rang out. She dropped behind a trunk and rested her head against the bark.

Logan sank behind the tree beside her, and Shadow curled in his lap. Even though the horses had run, they were in the open and worried her, but there was little she could do about that.

She closed her eyes. If she hadn't bent over at that moment, she'd be dead. She lifted a shaky hand and smoothed the hair out of her face. *Thank you, God, for protecting us.* Her eyes popped open. That was the first time in a long time she'd prayed without thinking about it. Was this how Logan felt in the proverbial foxhole?

"Are you hurt?" Logan's question yanked her from her thoughts.

"I don't think so. I'll let you know once my heart isn't in my throat."

He chuckled. "Got it."

"Who is this guy? First explosives. Now, a sniper? He has to be military."

"That wasn't a sniper."

She jerked her gaze to him. "Explain that."

"If that man was a sniper, you'd be dead." Logan shook his head while he ran a hand over Shadow's back. "I'd guess that guy's a hunter."

She sighed. "I suppose the knowledge of explosives could be related to a career as a blaster for a construction company or an oil and gas well perforator. That would track for around these parts."

"Exactly."

Her phone buzzed in her pocket. "Must be Mom." Izzie dug

it out and glanced at the caller ID. "Nope. It's Daniel." She answered it. "Hey, bro."

"Hey, yourself. What was that?"

"You mean the gunshot?"

"Yes." He drew out the word.

"Well, it was either a sniper with poor aim or our suspect taking target practice at us."

"Not funny, sis."

"What can I say? You're rubbing off on me."

Daniel grunted. "I'm calling it in. Are you safe?"

"For the moment."

"Stay there."

"Yes, sir." Had the man forgotten he worked for her and not the other way around?

As if sensing her ire, Logan reached over and clasped her hand. "Give the man a break. His sister was shot at."

"Yeah, what Logan said." Daniel must have heard Logan's response.

"Fine. You're forgiven."

"I'll let you know when it's clear."

"Thanks, Daniel."

He hung up, and she tossed the phone onto her lap. "Sorry."

"About what? You didn't tell the man to shoot at you."

She shrugged. Because of her the investigation was delayed. "You think he's gone?"

"I'm thinking no. Not yet."

Izzie puffed out a breath. "Come here often, soldier?"

"Sailor."

"Excuse me?"

"SEALs are sailors or operators, not soldiers."

"Okay, then. Come here often, sailor?"

He chuckled. "You really are channeling your inner Daniel."

"Meh. I tend to get weird when I get the living daylights scared out of me."

"That I can understand." Logan squeezed her hand.

"So where is this guy?"

"Behind you to your right on the ridge about a quarter of a mile away."

She peeked around the corner. "Are you sure he isn't a sniper?"

"Positive. That's not that far for a long-distance shot. He wouldn't have missed. Trust me. Snipers are accurate from eleven hundred yards or more."

"Well, there's that." Izzie's brain hurt. Not to mention her arms, legs, neck, face…okay, so everything ached.

The glorious sounds of sirens peppered the air.

"If the pattern holds of him bolting when he hears someone approaching—the guy is gone." Logan's finger circled in the air, indicating the deputy flying toward Stone Creek Ranch. "But let's wait for the all clear."

Thirty minutes later, her phone rang. She put it on speaker. "Did you find him?"

"No, but Deputy Wagner found the spot where he hunkered down. Unfortunately, there's no evidence other than a disturbance in the dirt."

"That figures. We'll head back to the house."

"Be careful, Izzie. We don't know if he moved, or if he's gone."

"Copy that. See you in a few." She disconnected the call. "Well, I guess we should go." Izzie didn't move. The thought of exposing herself out in the open sent dread rippling through her.

Logan stood and brushed off the seat of his pants then held his hand out. "Come on."

She accepted his gesture and used the tree for balance. Shadow snugged next to her. Hand on his back for stability, she took a deep breath, calming her nerves.

"Let me go first." Logan eased from where they'd taken up refuge. He scanned the distance. "I think we're good."

Izzie ducked under a limb and came to a stop by his side. She whistled. Firefly and Cricket appeared in the distance and trotted over. They nuzzled her neck, demanding pets. Shadow resumed his duty next to Logan. She ran her hands over the horses. "They look no worse for wear."

"At least they had the smarts to move away from danger." Logan took Cricket's reins and swung up in the saddle.

She followed his lead. "Time to put an end to this and figure out who's behind it all."

"I couldn't agree more."

"A quick shower since I look like I rolled in the dirt, then we go to the office and dive in." She tapped Firefly with the heels of her boots. The horse took off.

Logan and Cricket caught up with her.

She added speed to their trip to the barn. An open pasture wasn't on her favorites list at the moment. The emergency lights on the sheriff's vehicle blended with the sun. But knowing one of her deputies, along with Daniel, had eyes on the area eased her concern—a smidge.

Logan's countenance had changed. The warrior inside had come out to play. His eyes never stopped combing the perimeter of the ranch.

Funny. The man's protectiveness hadn't suffocated her. For the first time in a long time, Izzie felt safe letting someone—Logan—invade her independence.

She scanned the trees. Had the man left? Or was he watching and waiting for a new opportunity?

God, please keep us safe. And let us find the person responsible for abducting Lisa and killing those women. I can't handle failure in this case.

NINE

The conference room at the sheriff's office resembled an all-too-familiar tactical operations center he'd experienced as a SEAL. Logan leaned away from the large table, eyeing the photos on the wall. That morning's attempt on Izzie's life rattled him. Muscle memory had him responding to the threat, but the echo of the shot had wreaked havoc with his mind. He'd held it together, but the flashbacks threatened to emerge. Shadow had slept on his feet since they'd arrived, grounding him to reality and holding the memories at bay.

Shadow stood and stretched with a big groan. His nose nudged Logan's elbow, and he laid his snout on Logan's leg.

"Oh, so you want pets, huh?" He obliged his canine companion.

Izzie ambled in. Fatigue marred her features. "I've informed Cory we're hunkering down until we exhaust all possible connections and analyze the files which she acquired this morning." Izzie lowered herself onto an office chair, the aches from her injuries evident. "Daniel's bringing coffee and pastries from Saddle Sips. He'll be here soon. Cory promised to deliver lunch and dinner if needed. I want this case solved."

"Hello, you fabulous people. Your day just got better—I'm here!" Daniel stood in the doorway and raised a hand holding a bag of treats.

Izzie rolled her eyes. "Get in here, you goof."

Daniel strolled in and placed the beverage tray on the table along with the pastries. "What did I miss?" He took his cup and sat.

"We got the files you requested from Oklahoma and Arkansas about ten minutes ago. We haven't cracked them open yet." Logan tapped on the folders.

Daniel stuffed a bite of a strawberry-and-cream-cheese Danish in his mouth. "Le'sh geh to i' then," he mumbled around the pastry.

"Manners, dear brother." Izzie tossed him a napkin.

Daniel swallowed and wiped his mouth. "Overrated. Logan, Izzie, you're on." The man waggled his finger between them.

Logan handed the Oklahoma file to Izzie then opened the one from Arkansas. He scanned the document.

Izzie spoke up first. "Not much here. Two missing women, six months apart. Both barrel racers with brown hair and brown eyes. There's not an exact time when they disappeared, but it was around a rodeo. Local law enforcement found one body buried in a shallow grave by accident when the area flooded, eroding the soil." She rolled her office chair to the whiteboard and tacked the pictures up. "Similar to Carrie's discovery. The woman had on the remains of a dress."

"Any lead on the other woman?" Daniel asked.

"Not as of right now. That's the quick version. It'll take time to read more in-depth." She looked at Logan. "What do you have?"

He ran a finger down the document, hitting the highlights. "Same description of the three women from Arkansas. This guy definitely has a type." Logan moved to the photos. *Wow. Okay then.* "This is creepy."

"What?" Izzie and Daniel leaned forward and said in unison.

He would have chuckled at the choreographed response if the image in front of him hadn't knocked him sideways. "They found the one-room cabin where the women were held. No bodies, but the DNA from the blood evidence discovered confirmed that. The windows are boarded up. There's only one way in and out. It appears he shackled them to the floor with enough chain to walk around but never reach the door." He handed the picture to Izzie and Daniel. "Do you notice anything interesting about the inside of the cabin?"

Izzie's forehead scrunched. She lifted the image and narrowed her gaze. "It's clean, as in organized and perfect." She pointed to the curtains on the nonexistent windows. "The place is decorated like a house."

"I've never seen a hunting cabin like that before." Daniel scratched his jaw. "It looks like something from back in the day. You know, a June Cleaver thing."

"The perfect wife." Izzie deflated in her seat. "That's what it looks like."

"Unless our guy's obsessive-compulsive. That would explain the room." Logan studied the pictures. "But the dresses found on the women and those shackles?" He shook his head.

"So what? Are you saying he dresses them up, holds them hostage and *makes* them become Little Miss Perfect Wifey?" Daniel's question dripped with disdain.

"Maybe." His thoughts went to his sister. What was she going through right now? Did this maniac have her chained in a room? "I don't know these women, but I do know my sister. She dreamed of having a husband and family someday, and she wanted to be a stay-at-home wife and mom. But this." He tapped the photo. "This is a twisted fantasy."

Izzie sat up straight. "Gentlemen, we might have the key we're looking for."

Daniel's eyebrows rose. "Care to share with the class?"

"Logan hit it. It's a fantasy. The guy is creating his perfect wife. Now we just need to figure out why and who."

"Oh, that's simple. Not a problem there." Daniel puffed out a breath and shook his head.

Izzie backhanded him in the stomach. "Stop it. We have a way forward. And if I'm wrong." She tugged her bottom lip in her teeth. "Well, an educated guess is better than nothing."

Logan stroked Shadow's head. "I agree. Let's run with it and see where it leads. We might be off on motive, but the rest—I'd say hits the mark."

"Fine." Daniel tossed his pen on the table. "I'm in."

"Start with the suspects we have, and we'll work our way out from there." Izzie stared at the board. "Daniel, get me property records and any evidence found on the old cases. And double check any DNA left behind. Logan and I will check alibis on our current list and look into travel records."

"Got it." Daniel opened his laptop and focused on his work.

The three of them worked in silence for the next half an hour, adding details to the board and putting documentation in a digital file.

Izzie tapped the dry erase marker on her palm. "So, who's left on our list?"

Logan lifted a finger. "I'll take that one. We haven't eliminated Grey Chapman, Isaac Sample or Harvey Powers. The rest had alibis for at least two of the abductions."

"Is there a reason we aren't looking at women for these crimes?" Daniel stretched his arms above his head and arched his back. "Ah, that's better."

"Going with our theory that the person who attacked me is the same one who abducted those women, then it is most definitely a man." Izzie had considered a female, but her gut and experience with the creep said no.

"I had to ask."

She nodded. "As you should." Another consideration rattled in her head. "Are we overlooking others in the community?"

"Well, Keats seems to know a lot and would have access to all the rodeo information." Logan's gaze darted between her and Daniel.

"Maybe. He was there right after your encounter with Zeus," Daniel pointed out.

Izzie shook her head. "I really don't think he did this."

"What about the other men who board horses at the barn? They'd know the goings-on firsthand."

Logan's logic made her head hurt. "Tell ya what. Daniel, you interview Harvey Powers, and Logan and I will take Grey Chapman and Isaac Samples. If we eliminate them, then we'll widen the search to every man in Marshall County. At least those who have links to the rodeo."

"That's a bit extreme, but I get your point." Daniel rose. "Meet y'all back here in a couple of hours."

Her brother grabbed his Stetson and sauntered out of the room.

She shifted to Logan. "Ready?"

"When you are."

If none of these interviews panned out, Izzie had no idea what to do. She had to find Lisa. Fast.

Logan mulled over the information while he drove to the ranch where Isaac Samples helped train horses. He prayed one of the three men left on their list was the guilty party. If not, the investigation would drag on. Not because Izzie and Daniel hadn't tried. But because of the spread-out nature of the crimes and lack of evidence to point to the *who* in the case. They were definitely not shooting fish in a barrel. More like trying to find a specific needle in a stack of needles.

He parked his truck, and the trio got out.

Izzie pointed to the fenced-in area. "Looks like Samples is in the paddock. Let's go have a chat with him."

Dust kicked up under their boots as they made their way to the fence. Logan hated Izzie being out in the open. The pasture-land stretched far and wide. He clocked the closest buildings or objects to use for cover as soon as they arrived. To say he was itchy about her safety was an understatement.

"Isaac, may we have a word?" Izzie jerked her head to the side signaling for him to join them.

"Sure thing, Sheriff."

The man handed another ranch hand the reins of the horse he was training and jogged over to them. "What can I do for you?"

"We have a few questions about Lisa Russell."

Isaac lifted the front of his hat and wiped his brow before setting it back on his head. "What do you want to know?"

"Were the two of you dating?" Logan asked. He couldn't help the irritation lacing his tone.

"Dating? Nah. Sure, we went out a few times with the rest of the group but never dated."

"A few people seemed to think otherwise." Logan crossed his arms over his chest.

Isaac laughed. "They have it all wrong, man. We always went out with a group. My fiancée would kill me if I was seeing another woman."

"Fiancée?" Izzie's voice went up an octave. Apparently, she had no idea the man had a girlfriend let alone a fiancée.

"Yeah, Jennifer's in the army. Any down time I have, I've been eating up miles between here and the base. Her stint ends in a few months, and she's getting out. Plan to marry her as soon as that happens."

Isaac's boss waltzed over. "I can vouch for that. The guy's driving me crazy with wedding talk."

Samples's face turned all kinds of red. "Sorry, boss."

The older man slapped him on the back. "No worries, son. I'm happy to see you and that daughter of mine finally tying the knot."

Daughter. Well, okay then. Didn't see that one coming.

"Thank you for your time." Izzie shook the man's hand.

Logan did the same, and he, Izzie and Shadow headed toward his truck.

"That was sooo not what I expected."

"Me either."

"If his story checks out and he has an alibi for the dates in question, we can mark him off. At minimum, he lowers on our list."

Logan nodded. He put the truck in Drive and made a U-turn in the driveway. "Where to?"

"Chapman's off downtown."

"Got it." A little while later, he pulled into a parking space in front of Grey Chapman's office.

He held the door open for Izzie, then he and Shadow followed her to the front desk.

"Hi, Kristi. Is Grey around?" Izzie smiled at the administrative assistant.

"Sorry, Sheriff. I haven't seen him since yesterday morning."

"Is he on a business trip?"

Logan stayed as inconspicuous as possible and let Izzie do all the talking.

Kristi shook her head. "That's what's weird. He won't return my calls."

"Maybe he's out of cell phone range."

That got Logan's attention. He straightened. If the man had Lisa in an obscure location, he wouldn't have service.

"Thanks, Kristi. If you hear from him, please let him know I'd like to speak with him."

"Will do, Sheriff. Sorry I couldn't be of help."

Izzie nodded and motioned toward the door.

Back in Logan's truck, they headed back to the sheriff's office.

"That was odd." Izzie's forehead scrunched.

"What?"

"That Grey's administrative assistant had no idea where the man is."

"Maybe he had a business meeting out of town that he didn't tell her about."

"That's a possibility. Let's drive by his house. If his car is there, we can do a well visit. If not, we'll check in again tomorrow."

"Tell me where I'm going." Logan's mind ran wild. If the man was the killer, that would explain his absence and the lack of contact. He wanted to storm into the man's house. Grey could be holding Lisa while they had to play by the rules.

TEN

Two hours later, with no success finding Grey, Izzie sat at the conference room table, eyes closed. The day had thrown her for not only one, but multiple loops. Her head spun from the lingering headache and too much information.

"Sis." Daniel's quiet tone tugged at her.

She opened her eyes. "What's up?"

Her brother sat across from her. He hadn't been there a few minutes ago. She straightened. Had she fallen asleep sitting up?

"I just got here."

"Oh, okay. What did you find out from Harvey?"

Logan unsuccessfully tried to hide his smirk.

The weasel found it funny she'd zoned out and thought she'd fallen asleep. A smile tugged at her lip. It was kind of humorous.

"He didn't do it."

A yawn cracked her jaw. "What makes you say that?"

"Harvey said he got tired of his lingering depression, so he started seeing a therapist twice a week for the past two years. The therapist confirmed Harvey has never missed an appointment. Plus, about six months ago, he and Angelina Lopez started dating. The man is smitten. I also confirmed his alibi for a few other dates, and he checks out. Besides, Angelina doesn't fit the killer's type. It's not him."

"That narrows it down to Grey Chapman," Logan said.

"How so?"

"Isaac Sample checked out as well. But we can't get ahold of Grey, nor can Kristi." Izzie rubbed her eyes. She had to wake up. They had too much to do.

"I don't like the sound of that." Daniel tapped his pen on the table.

"Neither do we."

Logan pointed at her. "What she said."

Cory knocked on the door. "May I come in?" She held up a large brown bag.

Izzie sniffed the air and waved her into the room. "Smells amazing."

"I ordered from the Lazy Spur Café. Heath O'Brien delivered it a few minutes ago." Cory unloaded the containers and placed them on the table.

Logan took the one with his name on it. "I thought you said O'Brien was a livestock agent."

"Oh, he is, but he's helping Bonnie since she's shorthanded right now."

"That's nice of him." Izzie lifted the lid on her meal. Her stomach growled. "Guess I'm hungrier than I thought."

Cory laughed. "Enjoy. I'll see you tomorrow." The administrative assistant smiled, turned to leave and stopped. "By the way, Raymond Burke came by a bit ago. He made a few adjustments to the website and gave me the virtual tour."

Izzie pointed her fork at Cory. "I'm glad it was you and not me. I just want the thing to work, not know *how* it works."

The woman shook her head and closed the door behind her.

Daniel bailed soon after dinner to help at the ranch for a couple hours but promised to come back if they hadn't called it quits yet.

The hubbub of the sheriff's office had quieted. The change made Logan edgy. Why? He had no idea.

Izzie flopped back in her chair. "I feel like we are going in circles."

"Want to call it a night and start fresh in the morning?" Logan asked.

"Let's give it another hour or so unless we have an idea where to go next."

"Sounds like a plan." Logan glanced at Shadow snoring at his feet. The dog's presence eased the stress that came with the investigation.

After reviewing the suspect list for the third or fourth time, they still had nothing solid. Even the men they'd added to the list had been eliminated due to health, job or alibi.

Izzie stood, hands on her hips in front of the whiteboard, staring at the photos from the crime scene in Arkansas. She tapped on the image of the cabin. "It's an older place. Almost looks as though it was originally abandoned."

"Instead of a property our killer owns?"

"Maybe. Maybe not. I'm throwing more darts, hoping something will stick. We'll request the property records tomorrow." She spun. "As for the killer, we haven't made much progress with the *who*. What if we focus on the *where* and look into abandoned homesteads or hunting cabins?"

"That's an interesting idea." The concept rolled around in his head. "How many of those types of properties are around here?"

The crease between her eyes deepened as she studied the ceiling. "In Marshall County, I'm guessing about eight or nine if we include hunting cabins. Briar County, I'm not as familiar with, but toward this side of the county, I'd say maybe two or three. The rest of the area? I have no idea."

"I'm all for starting locally and moving outward."

"I'll grab a map and push pins. We can see if a pattern jumps out at us."

"I don't know about you, but I require another cup of coffee if we plan to continue." He stood and Shadow popped to his side.

Izzie tucked the flyaway strands of hair behind her ears. "More caffeine might get me through the next couple of hours."

He flicked his gaze to her face, then to her visible injuries. He closed his eyes. They'd pushed too hard. As much as he wanted—needed—to find his sister, he couldn't ignore that if they kept going without rest, they'd get sloppy and miss an important detail.

"Coffee, then one more hour."

Izzie scowled at him.

Hands up, he stalled her retort. "That was a strong suggestion. Sorry if it sounded like a command."

She stared at him for a moment then headed out of the door. "Come on."

He followed her toward the staff room.

A sharp crash came from his left followed by a thud and a loud pop.

"Izzie! Get down!" Logan dropped to the floor. Shadow lay next to him, growling.

Smoke filled the main room of the sheriff's office, and a fire crackled near where the device landed.

He had to get her out of the building. Now.

"Sue! Logan, we have to get Sue." Izzie coughed. Smoke coated her tongue, and the pungent odor of sulfur and burnt rubber made her throat scratchy and eyes water. Her night office clerk's desk sat near where the Molotov cocktail, smoke bomb or whatever had landed inside the sheriff's office main room.

Logan patted the air. "Stay here."

"No way, I'm coming with you." She refused to sit on the sidelines while someone else saved one of her own. The urgency to help had nothing to do with the gaslighting her ex had done. It had everything to do with her desire to protect her people.

"Stay close."

Izzie crawled behind him through the thick haze toward the small blaze. She lifted her neckline to cover her nose and mouth. The thin cloth helped but didn't relieve the bitter taste from the acrid air. The smoke seeped into the material, sending her into a round of coughs.

Logan's back arched and body shook from a coughing attack.

Fear crept up her throat that they wouldn't get to Sue. That they'd die from smoke inhalation. And most of all, they'd fail to solve the case and leave Lisa in the hands of a madman.

God, please give us strength and wisdom. Izzie had prayed earlier and more often in the past few days than she had her entire life. Life had a way of showing a person the important things.

"Sue, grab my hand." Logan encouraged the employee to come out from under her desk.

Izzie glanced at the blaze. The fire hadn't spread, but the smoke continued to thicken. She left Logan to his task and crawled to the wall where they stored the fire extinguisher and fire blanket. Grabbing the blanket, she hurried back and tossed it over the flames.

"Let's get out of here and call the fire department." Izzie hunched over, staying low, and led the way to the front door.

"Wait!"

She spun and found Sue had done the same. "Logan?"

"Something's not right." His eyes searched the room.

Izzie coughed. "We have to get away from the smoke."

"It's a setup."

"How do you know?"

"Call it a gut instinct." Shadow whined at Logan's side. "I know, boy, we're going." He waved for Izzie and Sue to follow.

Sue hesitated. She swung her gaze from Logan to the front door.

"I trust him with my life. Listen to him." Izzie nudged her employee toward Logan.

The three of them wove through the desks. The smoke had thinned but continued to choke them. When they reached the back hall, Logan motioned for them to enter the conference room. Once inside, he closed the door. He doubled over coughing.

Izzie wiped her eyes, which burned from the odor and smoke.

"Thank you." Sue collapsed onto a chair.

She patted her friend on the shoulder. "Are you injured?"

Sue shook her head. "I don't think so. Just rattled."

"I'm calling for help." Izzie coughed again and dialed the number for the fire department.

"Stay away from the windows. I don't trust that whoever tossed that smoke bomb into the office isn't out there watching and waiting." He closed the blinds and moved next to Shadow. The dog quivered at Logan's side. "It's okay, buddy. We'll have Payton give you some love when we get back to the ranch."

Izzie caught his eye and nodded. She made a mental note to call her sister once they secured the office.

"Rollins Fire."

"This is Sheriff Sinclair. An unknown suspect threw a smoke bomb through the window of the sheriff's office."

"Hold." The tapping of keys filtered over the line. "Help is on the way, Sheriff. Do you need medical?"

"Send paramedics. Smoke inhalation is a concern." She'd requested medical for Sue, not for herself or Logan.

"Done. Anything else?"

"That's all." Izzie hung up and dialed Deputy Bennett.

"Bennett."

"Jackie, I need a perimeter check around the office."

Boots pounded on the ground, and a car door slammed. "Talk to me, Sheriff."

Izzie explained the smoke and fire, and Logan's sixth sense about the person attempting to smoke them out of the building—literally. "We've taken refuge in the conference room. Fire is on the way."

"I'm on it. I'll call Vince and have RFD hold until we clear the area."

"That works." Izzie glanced at Sue. "Medical can wait."

"I'll be in touch." Jackie disconnected.

"Deputy Bennett is verifying the attacker isn't out there."

Logan's shoulders drooped in relief. "Good." He stroked Shadow's head. The dog had calmed down some. "I recommend that we postpone our investigation until tomorrow."

"I think that's a great idea." As much as she hated stepping away from the case, her body had hit its limits, and her brain wasn't any better.

A while later, Deputy Bennett gave the all clear. The firefighters confirmed the small blaze had been extinguished, gave them oxygen and declared them okay to go home. Jackie ushered Sue to her car, which left Izzie, Logan and Shadow sitting at the conference room table. She'd let her deputy deal with the evidence collection.

She looked up and spotted Daniel leaning against the door jamb. Her brother must have heard the radio chatter and hightailed it into town. "You know, for a sheriff, you can't seem to stay out of trouble." Daniel beamed with mischief.

"Ha ha. If y'all don't mind, I'd like to go to the ranch now."

Daniel pushed off the wall. "I'll escort you out there."

"Under normal circumstances, I'd argue. But after today, I'm all for extra protection."

"Mark this down in history, Logan. My sister, the big, bad sheriff, isn't rejecting my help." Daniel laughed like a loon.

Logan shook his head. "Come on, Shadow. Let's go see your favorite vet."

Izzie walked between the two men, grateful for the shelter they provided. She glanced at Logan and decided to risk her heart. She slipped her hand into his and laced their fingers together.

Logan squeezed. A smile bloomed on his lips.

For the first time in what seemed like forever, the thought of a relationship didn't send her into a cold sweat.

However, her attacker's ability to know where to find her… Panic clawed at her already scratchy throat.

ELEVEN

After a fitful night's sleep at the ranch, Logan sat at the kitchen table and sipped his coffee. The caffeine jolted his system awake. Izzie had headed to the barn earlier to help with the chores. She and Miss Hannah insisted he stay and take care of Shadow. The dog hadn't left his side since Payton cleared him healthwise last night. Logan hadn't fought his furry friend about sleeping on the bed. The exploding glass and smoke had him teetering on the edge of flashbacks. Even in Shadow's needy state, his canine companion performed his tasks like a pro, easing Logan's anxiety.

He took another sip and let the bold brew chase away the memories. Yesterday's events had Logan wondering, not for the first time, how the suspect knew where to find Izzie. He'd stake his reputation that the man wasn't prowling the town to find her. Not with the guy's fantasy in play—with Logan's twin no less. His jaw clenched. What had they missed?

God, please keep Lisa safe. Let us find her before it's too late. We need a clue. Just one that points us in the right direction.

"Morning." Daniel's sock-clad feet padded across the kitchen floor. Dirt clung to the thighs of the man's jeans. His friend had come from the barn and left his boots in the mudroom.

"Chores done?"

"Yup." Daniel poured a cup of joe and snagged a muffin from the plate on the counter.

Logan sat his mug on the table. "I feel like a slacker."

Daniel chuckled and dropped onto a chair across from him. "Nah. We have it down to a science."

"Where's Izzie?"

"Right here." She and Hannah joined them. "Just giving Firefly and Cricket a little extra love." Izzie washed her hands then joined them at the table.

"Izzie gave me a general rundown. Where do you plan to start today?" Hannah leaned against the counter, wiping her hands with a dish towel.

Izzie's fingers brushed his. The smile tugging at his lips escaped. The old Izzie had begun to shine. He'd noticed the transformation during their encounter with the smoke bomb. Her confidence had risen, and her willingness to let others step in and help hadn't stirred her anger.

Hannah's gaze landed on their hands. Her eyebrow arched.

Izzie ignored her mother's pleased expression. "There are several hunting cabins that I know of, but they're on owned land. I thought we'd hit the old Callahan place, Baker's, and Mueller's first. Those are the only abandoned properties I know of in Marshall County."

Deep in thought, Hannah's forehead scrunched. "That's all I can think of as well."

Daniel finished his coffee and pushed from the table. "I'll continue sifting through names and doing background checks while the two of you go fishing."

Izzie wadded up a napkin and threw it at her brother. "You do realize we might catch a big one while you swim aimlessly about?"

"Ha ha. Funny, you are not." Daniel picked up the paper and tossed it in the trash. "Call if you need backup."

"Will do." Izzie stared at her drink. "What do you think? Are we fishing?"

Logan glanced at Hannah, who was doing a great impression of a statue. "I think your suggestion of abandoned homesteads is valid and deserves attention."

"Thank you." She met his gaze, conveying an unspoken gratefulness for believing in her abilities.

His approval had bolstered her confidence. She was smart, strong and excelled at her job. Why her ex, Will, had said otherwise was beyond Logan. However, he'd quietly protect this woman with his life if it came down to it. "Shadow and I are ready when you are."

Shadow's head popped up from where it lay on his paws. Logan laughed at the dangling pink tongue and the pants that accompanied it. The dog's black eyes twinkled with excitement. One would think Logan had promised Shadow a steak.

"Give me twenty to clean up. Then we'll hit the Callahan place first and go from there." Izzie placed her cup in the sink and hurried from the room.

"I see you got her to talk."

Logan froze and shifted his gaze to Hannah. "What do you mean?"

"Even with everything that's happened and Izzie's stress over this case—specifically your sister—that girl is more at ease than I've seen her in years. More impressive, she cares about your opinion, and not from a place of self-doubt."

He wasn't convinced about the last part. He'd seen Izzie's need for affirmation, but he agreed with Hannah. Izzie's demeanor had changed for the better.

Hannah chuckled. "I can see you're not so sure. But when she didn't bite Daniel's head off when he suggested the two of you were chasing your tails, I call that a win. Whatever you did, keep it up." Hannah placed her hand on Logan's shoulder.

"I'm getting my girl back. And I have you to thank for that." The older woman left him alone with his thoughts.

Logan petted Shadow's head. "What do you think, my man? Do we follow these feelings once we find Lisa and risk rejection? I mean, she already knows my issues and hasn't told me to buzz off yet."

Shadow sat up and whoo-whoo'd.

"Yeah, I agree. Izzie's worth it." He scratched under Shadow's chin. "You give great advice."

"You're talking to your dog again." Izzie waltzed in with her black hair in a high ponytail and in her casual sheriff's look of jeans and a department polo. But that didn't detract from the air of authority that swirled around her. Hannah was right. Izzie *had* changed.

"He's a great sounding board."

"Does he talk back?"

"On occasion." Logan smiled. "Let's get moving and pray today's the day we find evidence of Lisa's location."

"Amen to that." Izzie snatched her sheriff's Stetson and his from the hook by the back door and handed him his hat. "Come on, you two. We're wasting daylight."

The three of them piled in Logan's truck and headed down the lane of Stone Creek Ranch.

"Okay, Miss Navigator, navigate." He placed his Stetson on the seat between them, retrieved his aviators from the sunglasses holder and slipped them on.

He felt Izzie's eye roll more than saw it. But he knew it was there.

"Take a left away from town. There's a county road a few miles up. Turn right at the large oak tree."

The Texas morning rose to greet them, and it didn't disappoint. The purple, pink and yellow spring flowers faced the sun in full color, and the trees worked hard on filling out. He'd missed his home state. But more than that, he'd missed Rollins.

Twenty-five minutes later, he pulled down the drive of an old farmhouse. Logan scanned the property. "Not much here."

"Old man Callahan died almost five years ago. His kids inherited the place but live in New York. Both work in the corporate world and don't care much about the farm their daddy purchased a decade ago after his wife passed away. He'd always dreamed of a small farm and decided to go for it." Izzie leaned forward and peered out the windshield. "I've always loved this old place. It looks like they hired someone to bushhog the front pasture and lawn at some point, or maybe a kind neighbor did it. It's not completely overgrown."

Logan parked near the farmhouse. "Where do you want to start?"

"House first, then the barn." She slid from the truck.

He opened the back door, and Shadow hopped out.

Shadow sat and barked, panting with excitement. He'd give the dog kudos for finding excitement in everything he did.

"Come on, boy." Logan climbed the five steps to the porch. Spiderwebs arched from one corner to the other. Dirt covered a dilapidated swing and the floor.

"I met Callahan's daughter for the first time at the man's funeral. I told her I'd keep an eye on the old place. She thanked me, then told me where to find the key and said I could drop by anytime." Izzie stood on her tiptoes and removed a small box from a hidden spot inside a column. "I drive by on occasion."

"You're not concerned she'll protest us entering the house since it wasn't recent?"

She shook her head. "I have it in writing back at my office." The door squeaked open, and they entered. Izzie waved a hand in front of her face and coughed. "It doesn't appear that anyone has graced the house in a long time."

Logan stepped around her and examined the interior. "I have to agree." A thick layer of dust covered the surfaces. The fine powder tickled his throat.

Shadow sneezed, tossed his head back and forth, and sneezed again.

"I agree, buddy. Someone needs to clean this place." The navy SEAL in him shuddered at the mess. "Why don't they sell it?"

"The man placed a condition in the trust that the family couldn't sell the property for five years after his death. I guess Mr. Callahan hoped his children would change their minds."

"Looking around this place, that answer is no." Logan inspected the old house. For being abandoned, it was still in great shape.

Ten minutes later, they headed toward the barn.

"How big is this property?" Logan scanned the land surrounding them.

"It consists of the farmhouse, barn and a shed for equipment. The entire place is about forty acres with pastures and woods beyond."

"Not enough for a ranch or a sizable beef farm, but decent for a hobby farm or general homestead."

"Unless one of the ranchers in the area wants to add on, it'll probably take a while to sell this place."

Logan loaded Shadow in the truck after they'd searched the barn. The only things alive on the property were a family of mice and a couple of raccoons.

"Where to next?" He started the engine and headed down the lane.

"The Baker farm is on the opposite side of town. Let's hit Mueller's place first. It's about ten minutes from here."

He followed her instructions. "What do you know about the family?"

"Not a lot. Mr. Mueller died several years ago. He left the place to his daughter Ellie. I've never met her, and as far as I know she's never set foot on the land."

"What's going to be your excuse to get in the house?"

"I'm searching for a killer." She shrugged. "The place is abandoned, and we're checking it out for safety purposes."

Logan glanced at her and raised a brow. "And that'll work?"

"Meh. But we're small-town Texas. No one should be on that property. The taxes are still paid through a trust from the older Mueller."

"So the daughter never collected her inheritance?"

"Not according to the estate attorney in charge of Mueller's affairs."

Logan approached the old farm and parked. "Well, it appears deserted." He pointed to the dirt path between the house and the barn. "However, that looks a little too smooth. Maybe Ellie *has* been out here."

"Doubtful. House first."

He joined Izzie at the front door. She tried the knob. When it turned, she drew her weapon. "That shouldn't have happened."

He held his personal gun at his side. Izzie had already given him a hard time about it, but he refused to go without a way to protect her. Although, he'd never admit that to her. "Clear the house?"

She nodded. "I'll go left. You go right."

"Shadow, stay."

Twenty minutes later, they stood in the living room, guns holstered.

Logan snapped his fingers, and his dog joined him at his side.

"Well that was anticlimactic. Not that I mind." Izzie laughed. She glanced at her watch. "Let's split up. I'll take the house if you'll explore the barn."

"Right." Logan struggled to keep the smirk off his face. "For a country girl, you sure do have a thing about mice."

She smacked his arm. "I can't help it. Those beady little eyes and teeth." Teeth over her bottom lip, she mimicked the creatures. She fake shivered. "Nope. You can have the little things."

Logan rolled his eyes. "Come on, Shadow. Let's go save Izzie from the big, bad rodents."

"Smarty pants!"

He chuckled as the front door closed behind him. However, the idea of splitting up had him questioning the plans.

"Shadow, how do I protect her without stomping on her independence, especially with her being the sheriff and all?"

The dog woofed and trotted along beside him.

As Logan approached the barn, his sixth sense kicked in. The one that had saved him and his team more than once, except for his last mission. His hand hovered over his weapon. Shadow detected his tension and plastered himself against Logan's leg.

He scanned the surroundings. Trees lined one side of the property and open pasture filled in the remaining space. Finding nothing, he eased open the door. Dust particles floated in the air, and a stale stench invaded his nose. Faint scrape marks trailed the dirt floor.

"Shadow, ears up." Logan pulled his SIG Sauer from his holster and held it next to his leg. The hair on his neck prickled.

The easygoing dog disappeared. Shadow snarled. A low growl rumbled from him.

Logan froze. Moving only his eyes, he examined the interior a second time. Something was off.

Shadow barked then raced across the barn and out the back door.

Logan resisted the urge to call his dog. He sprinted after Shadow. At the exit, he paused and peered around the corner.

Handgun ready, he moved toward a small patch of dirt beyond the barn where Shadow sat.

"Shadow?" Logan's gaze flicked toward the trees. No movement. "What is it, buddy?"

The dog pawed at the ground.

He took a closer look.

The shape of the bare spot clicked. A grave. But was it an animal or human?

* * *

Izzie wiped her finger along the fireplace mantel. A thick layer of dust clung to her skin. She spun and allowed her gaze to travel over the living room. A search of the kitchen had come up empty, same as the living room. A smile tugged at her lips. She'd thought Logan would for sure complain about splitting up the jobs, but to her surprise he hadn't balked. The fact they'd cleared the house before he'd headed to the barn had eased her worries. Although, she'd never admit it.

Maybe a relationship with the right guy wouldn't be so bad. She chuckled. Who was she kidding? Only one guy stood out. Logan. And the way he respected her and her job… Izzie exhaled. The weight of the past melted away. Her father's betrayal and Will's gaslighting had held her captive too long. She'd been so wrapped up in heartache that she'd refused to rely on God, for fear He'd let her down too. She should have known better. Her brothers had embodied pillars of strength and support. They'd stood by her in everything she'd done.

Well, no longer would she allow her father and Will to taint her future.

God, I'm fully and truly back. I'm sorry for keeping You at arm's length. Thanks for being patient with me and for sending Logan to show me a man can be protective and respect me for who I am.

She ambled to Mr. Mueller's office. Papers sat stacked on one side of the desk. She turned in a circle, taking in the space. It looked as if he'd be back any minute, if not for the layer of dust and stale air.

A planner sat on the desk, stuck in time. Curiosity got the best of her. She flipped the pages of the time capsule. Her phone buzzed in her pocket. She pulled it out and answered it without looking. "Sheriff Sinclair."

"Hey, sis." Daniel's less than chipper tone had her straightening.

"What's wrong?" She peeked at the papers but nothing important jumped out. After one last look, she moved to the primary bedroom.

"I'm going through old records and ran across something I think you need to take a look at."

A picture frame graced the top of the dresser. She picked it up. Mr. Mueller and a young boy stared back at her. The two resembled each other. She squinted at the image. Who was this little boy? The man didn't have any grandsons.

"Sis?"

"Sorry. What were you saying?" Maybe if she took out the picture it would have names written on the back. She brought the image closer before flipping it over. "We're at Mueller's old farm. I got preoccupied by an interesting photo I found."

"Mueller's daughter had a child."

"We know that. She has three girls."

"No, Izzie. Before that. She had a previous marriage and child."

Izzie jerked her head up. "How do you know that?"

"I discovered old documents from when he lived in Oklahoma. It took some digging, but his daughter up and left her husband and their son."

"Go on."

"Ellie's first husband was a bronc rider in his day, and she was a barrel racer. She left without looking back, and her ex became a drunk and abused their son."

"Daniel, what are you trying to tell me?"

She placed the photo on the dresser and moved to the closet. Dresses in different sizes lined the rod. A pile of clothes sat in the corner. Izzie knelt and lifted the shirt on top. A pair of jeans were next.

"Izzie, old man Mueller's grandson—we know him."

She recognized the outfit and gasped. Lisa's.

"Izzie? Izzie! What is it?"

"Dresses. And Lisa's clothes."

An explosion rocked the house. Windows shattered and threw her to the floor. Her phone clattered against the hardwood. Drywall particles floated in the air, choking her.

She staggered to a stand and scurried across the broken glass to where the window used to be. A dark haze blocked her view. The smoke dissipated, and she got her first view of the barn. Or where the barn once stood. "Logan?" A sob stuck in her throat. Tears blurred her vision.

Broken boards scattered across the yard, and flames snaked toward the sky.

God, please don't let Logan and Shadow have been in there.

The pounding in her chest threatened to crack her rib cage. If Logan was alive, she had to call for help. She pushed from the wall and stumbled toward her phone. The blast had messed with her inner ear, throwing off her balance.

The floor creaked behind her. Logan. He must have left the barn before the explosion. She turned.

Izzie stared at the hardwood. Debris poked her palms. Crimson droplets splattered the floor. She blinked, trying to clear her head.

On all fours, she lifted a hand to her throbbing cheek. She hadn't fallen. Someone had hit her. Her blurry gaze landed on the person responsible, but she couldn't see him through the ski mask.

Her phone lay several feet away. Had it disconnected? Would Daniel know to send help? She had to survive and find a way to help Logan, assuming he survived the blast.

"Daniel!"

"Oh no you don't." Hands grabbed her and tossed her against the wall.

Izzie fought the pain threatening to incapacitate her. She slid her hand behind her back and wrapped her fingers around the grip of her Glock.

"Now, now, Sheriff. I can't let you do that."

Her reaction time too slow, her attacker grabbed the gun and tossed it aside.

With all the energy she could muster, she reached out and yanked the mask from his head. Her breath stuttered. "You?"

"Too bad you didn't mind your own business, Sheriff." The title oozed with disdain. His arm circled her neck. "Nighty night." A needle pierced her skin, and she collapsed. A black abyss sucked her in.

Logan, I'm so sorry.

At least she'd gotten right with God.

The world fell away.

TWELVE

Something wet tickled Logan's cheek. He swatted it away, but the sensation didn't stop. He cringed at the ringing in his ears and lifted his hands to press over them. His fingers brushed against fur. He blinked. Shadow's black eyes stared at him. The dog's nose, inches away from his. What had happened? Shadow licked his face. He ran his hand over the canine's neck and searched his brain. The grave. The explosion.

Logan sucked in a breath, rolled to his side and pushed up to a seated position. The world chose that moment to go on a merry-go-round ride. He grabbed his head and blew out air between pursed lips.

Shadow whined next to him.

"I'm okay, boy." Maybe. Nausea swirled in his belly. He'd always hated the tilt-a-whirl at the carnival. His head had decided to take an extended ride. He had to find Izzie and make sure the blast hadn't hurt her. Logan staggered to a stand, using Shadow for stability.

His gaze swept the property. Pieces of boards scattered the ground and tentacles of flames slithered skyward. If Shadow hadn't brought him to the grave and far enough away from the point of detonation, he'd be dead. He owed the furry guy a big juicy steak for saving his life. His eyes drifted to the farmhouse. The windows had shattered, and debris lay on the porch.

The explosion must have scrambled his brain. Izzie should have come running once the dust settled. Where was she?

"Come on, Shadow." Logan straightened, shoved aside his aches and pains, and concentrated on each step as he strode across the yard. Her SUV had been pummeled, and pieces of wood lay on top of it. "Izzie!"

When silence met his ears, worry took root in his gut. He quickened his pace and stumbled his way to the porch. "Izzie?" The front door stood open. He unholstered his SIG Sauer and stepped inside. A wave of dizziness washed over him. He placed a hand on the wall and inhaled. His head didn't hurt like he'd hit it. Most likely his inner ear had gone wonky with the blast.

His phone buzzed. He pulled it out of his pocket and answered. "Hello."

"Logan, where's Izzie?" Daniel's frantic tone chased away the remaining cobwebs.

"I'm not sure."

"What do you mean you don't know?" His friend shouted the question.

Logan flinched. "Daniel, tone it down. My ears are still ringing from the explosion."

"What?"

Oh, yeah, the man didn't know. "The barn blew up."

"I'm three minutes out."

He brought the phone down and looked at it then moved it back to his ear. "Why? No, wait. I'm glad, but how are you so close?"

"I was on the phone with Izzie when she was attacked."

"Whoa. Back up. What happened?"

"Logan, are you okay?"

"I think so. Now, tell me what you meant." He stepped inside and cleared one room after another until he came to the bedroom. Izzie's gun lay near the far wall. Pieces of glass littered the floor. The appearance of a scuffle had his heart rate skyrocketing. He commanded Shadow to sit by the door. He didn't want the pooch to get glass in his paws.

The front door banged open. "Logan!"

"In here, Daniel."

Shadow growled.

Daniel skidded to a halt at the doorway. "Want to call off your dog?"

"Shadow, chill. You know him. Sorry, Daniel. He must be a bit shaken."

As if on cue, Shadow panted and tilted his head with a doggy smile in place.

"Guess I can't blame him after what I saw was left of the barn. Did you find Izzie?"

"Not yet. But from what it looks like…" Words refused to come. He pointed at the blood drops and the smeared dust and glass. "You were on the phone with her?"

Daniel nodded. "I called to give her new information. Before I could say anything, she found a framed picture and dresses, including Lisa's clothes in the closet."

"Are you kidding me?" Logan's heart jumped to his throat.

"I searched the rest of the house before I made it to the bedroom. But she hasn't answered my callouts." Logan moved to the closet. His gaze slid to the floor. "Daniel!"

The man rushed to join him. "What?"

He picked up the clothes lying on the floor then pointed to the dresses.

"These look like what Mom would have worn years ago."

Logan nodded his agreement. "Does it remind you of the one on Carrie's body?"

"It does. Let's find that picture Izzie talked about then I have things to tell you."

Logan found the photo where it had landed on the floor and

slid under the bed. He got on his hands and knees, stretched to reach the frame, then scooted back. "Got it."

Daniel moved next to him and studied the image. "That's Mr. Mueller. The kid…" The man exhaled. "I'm assuming it's Mueller's grandson."

Logan's mind screamed to bolt out of the house and search for Izzie, but the SEAL in him demanded he slow down and gather intel and make a plan. He now understood why people ran off halfcocked when a loved one was in danger. If he didn't let his training kick in, he'd fail the woman he'd come to love. Yes, loved. He'd never stopped. But could he be the man to stand beside her? Fill her with the self-confidence that had been destroyed? He wasn't sure, but he wanted to try.

"That's why I called Izzie. I ran across interesting information about old man Mueller. He has a grandson, and we know him." Daniel walked out of the room.

Logan swallowed his protest—to finish the discussion here and now—and followed his friend with Shadow pushing against his leg.

Daniel took a seat in the living room. "I thought you could use to sit before you fell down."

"I'll admit my ears are still a bit wonky." *Tell me what you know!* Logan inhaled to get his runaway thoughts under control.

"Mueller used to live in Oklahoma before he moved here. As I was telling Izzie, his daughter Ellie was a barrel racer. From what I discovered, she left her husband and son for another man. The ex-husband turned into a drunk. The boy suffered because of it."

"You believe the divorce sent her son over the edge, and he became obsessed with women? More specifically barrel racers that reminded him of his mother?"

"No, I think his mother having a wonderful other family is what did it. But yes. I think Heath O'Brien is living out the perfect wife fantasy." Daniel bounced his foot. The man was itching to go as much as he was. But they had no direction yet.

"If it's him, how does he know where Izzie is all the time?"

"Heath's been delivering meals to the sheriff's department from the café. Maybe he's listening in."

"So what? He can't hear everything. He's not there all the time."

"So much for that idea."

The pieces clicked into place. "Unless someone bugged the office."

Daniel's head whipped up. "Say what now?"

"He seems to know where Izzie is. When he shot at us at the ranch, Izzie had called in and told Cory she'd be late because of the fence."

Daniel scrubbed his face. "How did we miss that?"

"It wouldn't be hard. He comes and delivers food and hangs out. Cory leaves the room, and he slips a listening device under her desk or somewhere in the main room. A great way to find out about all kinds of things."

"I'll have Deputy Wagner sweep the office." The man tapped out a text message.

"What about the experience with explosives?" The theory sounded right, but not all the parts had fallen into place.

"We'll have to do a bit more digging, but my gut says we're on the right track." Daniel stood.

"With the evidence around us, I agree." Logan pushed to his feet. "Let's go figure out where Heath took Izzie and find Lisa in the process."

"From your lips to God's ears."

"Shadow, come." The trio strode outside, jumped in Daniel's truck and headed to the sheriff's office.

Logan stared out the window and tried to calm his racing nerves, but failed in a spectacular fashion.

God, I could use Your wisdom right now. Please let us find both of them before it's too late.

* * *

Izzie jolted awake. She bounced and smacked her head. Another bounce sent her into a hard surface. She whimpered. Zip ties held her wrists together. A rough carpet chafed her arms and cheek. Her body lay over a small hump. The hard mound dug into her side. A scratchy old blanket covered her. Where was she? The back seat of a truck or SUV? Or maybe the trunk of a car. She raised her hands. No. She had space above her. It had to be a back seat. Now that she had that dialed in, the next question…what happened? She searched her mind, but the lingering haze refused to lift. *Come on, Izzie, think.* Her eyes drooped closed. Why was she so tired? The rocking back and forth tugged her toward sleep.

"Get up."

The cover was yanked away. A harsh ray of sunlight sliced through her head. Her eyes slammed shut. A dull ache pulsed behind her lids.

"I said get up." The backlighting of the sun obscured the man's face. His large hands wrapped her bicep and yanked her from the vehicle.

Unable to get her feet under her, she fell to the ground. The gravel ripped a hole in the knees of her jeans and pierced her palms where she'd tried to catch herself. "Why are you doing this?"

He lifted her and tossed her toward the dirt path.

She struggled to remain upright. She glanced up at her attacker and recognized him immediately. Heath O'Brien.

"Now, walk." Heath pointed toward a cabin.

She drew several deep breaths and stumbled toward the small building. The brain fog dissipated with the fresh air. The picture and dresses in Mueller's house. The explosion. The struggle. All flooded back. *Oh, no. Logan. Please, God, let Logan and Shadow be alive.* She let the memories settle in. Daniel would send help. Unless her phone had disconnected, he'd heard her battle with the man behind her.

Her mind cleared, and she mulled over how to proceed. Woods surrounded the secluded cabin. She had no idea where in the county he'd taken her. For all she knew, they could be in another region of Texas. But she doubted it. Assuming the man's pattern held, they remained in Marshall or Briar County.

"Get inside." The guy pushed her toward the front door.

She fumbled with the knob and opened it. Stepping inside, she froze. The interior, a replica of a perfectly maintained home, unfolded in front of her. The only odd thing out of place—a cuff and thick chain attached to an anchor in the middle of the floor.

"Sit down and don't move." He shoved her onto the couch. A gun appeared that she hadn't noticed before. "Put the cuff on your ankle."

Izzie stared at the metal restraint. The back of the man's hand connected with her cheek, and she toppled to the side. She righted herself. Her face stung and tears welled in her eyes. Without further prompting, she did what the man asked.

"Good girl."

She bit back her response to his condescending tone. "Why are you doing this?"

If it were possible, his malicious glare would have sliced her to shreds. And the man's exasperated sigh would have been funny if she wasn't at his mercy.

He studied her for a moment, and as if a switch had flipped, he smiled. "I hadn't intended for you to join me. You're not like her." He lifted a piece of her hair and rolled it between his fingers. "Black hair. Maybe you'll be better."

"Like who?" Izzie thought about the picture she'd found and their theory about his fantasy. He had to be talking about his mother.

"Good wives don't ask questions." Heath took off her boots and placed them nicely and neatly on the shoe rack. He added his alongside hers. When he returned, he cut the zip ties off her wrists then lowered onto the recliner. "You're home now. If you're good, you'll stay. If you disappoint me—well, let's not talk about that yet."

"I don't understand." The cuff squeezed her ankle. Maybe it hadn't, but panic crept in. She kicked her foot.

"Don't talk back." A slimy smile crossed his lips. One that made her stomach roil. "Perfection takes time. I can be patient, but don't test me." He grabbed the chain and yanked.

The metal cut into her skin. Tears pooled on her lashes.

Heath stood and rounded the couch. He clutched a strand of hair and let it fall through his fingers. "Shh… Don't fight. You'll ruin everything. I've given you a new life—one where you don't have to make any choices."

She sat motionless, not wanting to provoke him or lead him on.

He leaned in. His hot breath against her ear sent a chill down her spine. "I know what's best for you. You'll learn in time. All the others did…at first."

Izzie jerked at the sharp pinch on her neck. The room rippled in waves. Nausea whirled in her belly. Her eyes grew heavy.

Heath had drugged her again. *Logan, I need you. Please find me.*

She fought the effects of the drug but failed.

What plans did Heath have for her?

God, help me.

THIRTEEN

Eighteen hours and no Izzie. Logan tossed his pen on the table and covered his face with his hands. Shadow had worked overtime calming him. His anxiety had spiked several times, and he'd struggled to control it. If his dog hadn't grounded him throughout the night, Logan might have stroked out by now. Knowing the *who*, but not the *where* was killing him.

"We'll find Izzie and Lisa. The alternative isn't an option." Daniel dropped onto a chair.

"But you haven't found Lisa in two months." Okay, so maybe that wasn't fair, but it was true.

"We had nothing to go on until Rex Hensen discovered Carrie's body." Daniel's shoulders drooped. His normal jovial tone had disappeared. "It can't be that hard to identify locations now that we know who's behind the abductions."

"It wasn't an accusation. I'm just frustrated." He felt bad for adding to his friend's distress. "And you're right—in theory."

Daniel waved him off. "I get it. I really do." The man sighed and leaned forward, resting his elbows on the table. "We're at a standstill until we get a hit on possible properties linked to Heath."

"At least we know it's not his father. The man lived in Oklahoma and died a penniless drunk. That's a dead end." Logan cringed. "No pun intended."

"That's usually my MO." Daniel's smile faded, and he ran

his hand through his hair. His sister missing was taking a toll on the man. "That leaves Heath's mother's side of the family."

Logan closed his eyes. "And we're sure it's Heath and not Raymond Burke, the web designer? He had access to the office." He felt like a cat chasing a laser beam. Pouncing on a clue only to discover it wasn't there.

"You've seen the evidence. And it will take a while to process fingerprints and DNA on the bug Wagner found under Cory's desk."

"True. I just don't want to be wrong." They'd studied the documents and researched Heath, confirming their suspicions. But the thought of focusing in the wrong direction caused his stomach to roil. They didn't have time to make a mistake. He worried they were too late for Lisa, and he refused to lose Izzie as well.

"We've answered all our questions, including the experience with explosives." Daniel tapped one of the folders. "Heath worked a short stint in the oil fields to get away from his father. According to his boss, he assisted the well perforator. He learned about explosives on the job. Between that and online research, he'd have the ability required to create a bomb."

"You're right. I'm grasping." His hand found its way to Shadow. "How did we miss Heath in the investigation?"

"We didn't. He made the secondary list that had links to the rodeo. But our attention went to others since Heath didn't fit our criteria because we had no clue about his past."

"Now that we know, it completes the puzzle."

"Any more doubt?"

Logan shook his head.

A knock on the door to the conference room had them both swiveling their chairs. "Hey, boys. I think I found something." Cory held a piece of paper in her hand. The woman had jumped in to help the moment she discovered Izzie had gone missing.

"Come on in." Daniel pointed to a seat next to him. "What do you have?"

Cory sat on the edge of the chair. "Now that the county property records office is open for the day, I received the documents we requested."

Logan scooted forward. "So, Heath O'Brien owns land around here?" *Please say yes.*

"Not exactly."

"Cory," Daniel warned.

"Keep your pants on. Nothing came back on Heath or the older Mueller. But I got to thinking. The trust holds Mueller's property, so maybe another location was similar."

"And?" Logan prodded. Izzie's and Lisa's lives didn't have time for Cory to take her Texas sweet time.

"And…" She drew out the word. "Mueller moved to Rollins for another reason. His granddaddy on his mother's side has history here. The granddaddy owned a cabin with hunting acreage on the border of Marshall County. The inheritance is under a trust with terms identical to Mueller's. These people had family money. I'll let you investigate that piece if you find it necessary." Cory's eyes pleaded. "Do you think she's there?"

"We can hope and pray." Logan tamped down his urge to run out the door. "Thank you, Cory."

The woman wiped a tear from her cheek and exited the conference room.

"Time for a plan." Daniel's fingers flew over the laptop keyboard.

Logan skirted the table and sat in the seat Cory vacated.

Daniel shifted the computer for him to see the map he'd brought up. "This is the area Cory's search indicated. There's no route to the Mueller cabin except for the main path straight to the property. He'd see us on approach."

Logan studied the map and pointed to the other side of the property. "What's over there?"

"A dirt road at the back of Mr. Gordon's farm. We could climb Gordon's fence."

"That's where we go in. Heath won't be expecting anyone from that direction." Logan continued to examine the map. He'd prefer two more plans, but without taking the time for recon, they'd go in with what they had. Izzie and Lisa couldn't wait. *God, let them both be there and alive.*

Daniel popped the laptop shut. "I'll call Gordon on the way so he doesn't shoot us."

"It would be funny if it wasn't true." Wouldn't that just top off the last twenty-four hours.

His friend slapped him on the back. "Welcome back to small-town Texas, Mr. Operator."

They hustled out to Daniel's truck. Shadow hopped in the back, and Logan buckled in the front passenger seat.

Hang on, Izzie and Lisa, we're coming.

Logan stared at the passing scenery. He and Daniel had made a lot of assumptions. First that Heath had taken Izzie to that cabin, and also, the biggest one of all, that Lisa was there as well and alive.

God, don't let us be wrong about this. Because if we are, I have no idea where to go from here.

The dress Izzie had been instructed to put on reminded her of something her mother would have worn years ago. And the bare feet in the kitchen—degrading. She'd hoped playing along would give her a clue to Lisa's whereabouts, but so far—nothing. Thankfully, Heath hadn't done anything inappropriate. He seemed more fixated on how she served him and the minuscule amount of food he'd allowed her to eat.

The perfect little wife. She snorted. Yeah, she didn't have a submissive bone in her body. Izzie peered over her shoulder from the sink, where she was doing dishes, confirming Heath hadn't heard her. His fist had found her face twice thanks to the lack of a filter on her mouth. Her fear shot up yesterday when she'd sat alone with him as he scrutinized her every action.

Last night, while Heath slept in the bedroom, she'd lain on the couch chained to the floor and had a long talk with God. After all these years, it had taken a madman abducting her for her to give her anger and self-doubt over to Him. The weight that lifted—enormous. Of course, she'd discovered the freedom now since she couldn't do anything about it.

For the first time in forever, so it seemed, she wanted to crawl up on God's lap and snuggle in like she used to do as a child with her father.

Wow, just look at her having a silent conversation with herself. Izzie rolled her eyes.

"Are you done yet?" Heath stomped to her side.

"Almost." Izzie took a cleansing breath and placed the last plate in the dish strainer. "Done."

He glared at her.

What had she missed? She scanned the sink and counter.

"You're not going to leave them there, are you?" He pointed to the dishes she'd just washed.

"Of course not." She cringed at the thought of him teaching her a lesson. Izzie grabbed the towel, dried the dishes and put them away. Making sure nothing was out of place, she turned to him. "Finished."

A series of beeps came from the other room. "Go sit." Heath pointed to the couch and stormed off to his bedroom.

Izzie lowered onto the cushion and rubbed her ankle where the metal cuff had chaffed it. Funny how *giving it to God*, as the saying went, had provided her with a new perspective. Couple that with her law enforcement background, if she found an opening, she'd take it. But until then, she'd glean as much information as possible and pray he'd lead her to Lisa. Because if Heath's pattern held true, he'd left Lisa to starve to death.

She studied the interior of the cabin once again. The windows had boards over them. The chain allowed her access to the kitchen, living room and bathroom. The front door remained out of reach. The man had done his homework.

The bedroom door banged open. The fury in Heath's gaze set every one of her nerves on edge. He unlocked the cuff on her ankle.

"Get up!" He aimed a handgun at her head. A Smith & Wesson by the looks of it.

Something had changed. The deranged look in the man's eyes and in his actions scared her.

Following his directions, she stood.

"Move!" He jammed the barrel of the weapon into her back, forcing her toward the door.

She slowed, mentally recording her surroundings.

"Don't tempt me." He clocked the back of her head with the barrel of the gun.

Stars burst behind her eyes. She stumbled down the two steps of the cabin and caught herself before she face-planted on the ground.

"You stupid…" His voice trailed off. He grabbed her arm and squeezed.

Izzie couldn't control the whimper that escaped.

He shoved her toward an outbuilding and flung open the door. "Get in."

The heavy beat of her heart stole her breath as she followed his directions. She blinked, willing her eyes to adjust to the dimly lit room.

"Down the stairs." He propelled her toward the other side of the structure.

What stairs? Her eyes darted around the tiny room.

"Don't make me hit you again."

"I'm sorry, but I don't see—"

He grabbed her by the hair and shoved her face into a panel. "Here." He slid back the panel and forced her into the opening.

Izzie slipped down a few stairs before righting herself. If

she'd have tumbled to the bottom, she might have broken her neck. The stairwell led to an underground hallway with a door on the right.

Heath aimed his gun at her and unlocked the door. "Move."

Sweat beaded on her forehead and her pulse raced. "Please don't leave me down here." She hated cellars. The things that skittered in the dark made her skin crawl.

An evil laugh echoed in the small space. With one hard push, she fell into the room onto her hands and knees. Panic slithered up her throat. A tiny lamp in the space gave her a modicum of relief. The door slammed, and the lock engaged. She dropped her head. How would she get out of here?

"Izzie?" A faint voice filtered through her worry.

She lifted her head and squinted. A woman lay on a thin mattress ten feet away. Izzie sucked in a breath. "Lisa?"

"Yes." Tears streamed down her friend's face. Lisa had lost weight. Her gaunt face spoke of a hard two months.

"I'm so sorry I didn't find you sooner." Izzie moved to her friend's side and clasped her hand. Tears filled her eyes. "I never stopped looking. I just didn't have anything to go on."

"I know you did everything you could." Lisa struggled to sit up.

"The guys are working on finding us." She hoped. Oh, how she hoped they'd figured out who had kidnapped her and where to look.

"Guys?"

"Daniel and Logan."

"Logan's here?" Lisa sobbed the question.

"Oh, honey. He's worried about you. He's been helping me investigate." Izzie brushed the hair from Lisa's forehead. "We've been worried about you. Did Heath hurt you?" Okay, so that was a stupid question.

"At first, until I gave in to his expectations. As long as I did what he told me, he never laid a hand on me."

"How long have you been down here?"

"Since a couple of nights ago, I think. It's hard to know night from day with no window. He forced me into this room and hasn't come back."

A scratch on the door grabbed her attention. She rushed over. "Hello!"

"No one is going to save you." Heath's cold voice sent shivers up her spine. "In fact, say your prayers because you're going to need them in an hour."

"Why?"

"You'll never know what happened. Oh, and by the way, I wouldn't recommend jiggling the door." His evil laugh penetrated through the wooden barrier then faded into the background.

Knowing the man's propensity for explosives, she had a good idea what he'd done. Izzie put her back against the wall and slid to the floor.

Logan, we need you. I need you.

She closed her eyes and prayed the guys made it in time.

"Do you have eyes?" Logan crouched next to Daniel concealed in the brush some sixty feet beyond the cabin nestled in the trees. The outside appeared worn and basic. But as the saying went, appearances could be deceiving, at least based on what they'd found in Arkansas. The hours since the barn explosion and Izzie's abduction had gutted him. The guilt and failure had come close to consuming him. If not for Shadow and his talks with God, he'd be a heap of a mess puddled on the ground.

Daniel lowered the binoculars and handed them to Logan. "No movement. But that doesn't necessarily mean anything. The windows are boarded."

"No car or truck. Do you think we're wrong about the location?" He visually searched the property.

"Either that or the critter cam we found at the property line alerted Heath, and he left."

"Check out that outbuilding."

"Not much there. What is it, eight by eight maybe?"

"That would be my guess." Logan placed his hand on Shadow's head. A simple touch settled his mind and body. "Plan?"

"You're the SEAL."

"And *you're* the deputy."

Daniel smirked. "Neither one of us wants to make a mistake."

"Amen to that, brother." He inhaled and slowly emptied his lungs. "We can't sit here forever, and we can't sneak in. I say go in strong and pray."

"I like your style." Daniel tucked the mini binoculars in his tactical pants. "Show time." He unholstered his Glock and rose.

Logan matched his friend's actions. Shadow stood, waiting for a command. "Ready?"

"Let's do it." Daniel hunched and sprinted toward the cabin. The man had skills that would do the Navy SEALs proud.

Logan hit the small porch at the same time as Daniel. They plastered themselves on opposite sides of the door.

Daniel glanced over and raised a questioning brow.

Logan nodded.

His friend slipped to his knee and picked the lock.

Logan held back the laugh threatening to burst out. Busting the door down, he was familiar with. Picking a lock? Not so much.

Standing with his hand on the knob, Daniel jerked his head toward the door.

Go time. Logan listened then signaled his friend to open the door.

Daniel went low, and he went high. They cleared the one-bedroom structure in no time.

Logan pointed to the screen in the bedroom. "He saw us coming."

Daniel nodded and both men returned to the living area and took in the details of the room.

"What on earth?" Daniel's fist went to his hip as he stared at a thick chain anchored into the floor.

The attached cuff had brown spots on the edges. Dried blood if Logan were to guess. Anger seeped into his veins at images popping into his mind. Failing Izzie—and the guilt of not finding Lisa—would destroy him.

"Look at this place."

"Trust me, I see it." He couldn't restrain the low growl in his throat. Shadow sat at his feet and tilted his head as if to ask, *Did that come from you?*

Daniel had missed the frustration in his tone, or the man chose to ignore it. "I feel like I tumbled into a fifties sitcom."

"It does have that vibe, but without the humor." The decor was all wrong for that decade, but the mindset was similar. "The bottom line is she's not here."

"The outbuilding?"

"What do we have to lose?" Except time.

They strode to the tiny structure on the edge of the clearing, approaching it with the same caution as they had the cabin. Once inside, Logan inspected the room. "Not much here."

Shadow ambled in behind them. His nose went up, sniffing the stale air. The dog moved to the opposite side and pawed at a panel.

"What's up with him?"

"I'm not sure. But one thing I've discovered since I got him is to listen to him. That dog has a sixth sense." Logan joined his dog and examined the wall. "There's a door here." He lifted his SIG Sauer as Daniel did the same with his Glock. "Shadow, get back." Logan snapped his fingers and pointed to a spot next to him. The dog sat dutifully where he'd signaled.

"In three." Daniel's gaze met his. "Three, two, one."

Logan flung the door open. A set of stairs greeted them.

"A root cellar?" Daniel flicked his gaze from the dark hole to him.

Shadow barked and bounded down the steps.

"Shadow!" Logan hissed. Barking continued from below.

"You don't think, do you?" The panic on Daniel's face mimicked Logan's.

"I—" He shook his head. "I'm not going there. I can't." Logan retrieved a flashlight from his pocket and took the lead. At the bottom, he came to an abrupt halt. The sight stole the air from his lungs.

"What is it?" Daniel joined him. "Oh."

"Logan?" Izzie's voice came from the other side of the door that Shadow had found. The one wired with explosives and a timer that read fifteen minutes.

"Izzie, stay back."

"I know. Heath implied he'd rigged the door."

"Are you okay?"

"That's relative." He heard her chuckle. "Oh, and I found your sister."

"You what?" He froze. His heart rate spiked.

"Hey, Logan." Lisa's weak words were the most glorious thing he'd heard in a long time.

"Hi, sis." His throat clogged with emotion.

"Yo, Logan. I hate to break up the reunion, but that thing isn't gaining time." Daniel pointed at the device on the door.

He shifted his attention to the red numbers. Twelve minutes. Could he do this? He wiped his sweaty palms on his jeans. Shadow whined and pushed against him. Hand on the dog's head, Logan aimed the flashlight at the bundle of wires. The memories of the bomb that killed Monty and buried him in debris tore through his mind.

"Logan?" Izzie pulled him from the flashback.

Shadow tugged on the hem of Logan's shirt.

He forced himself from the deluge of images. "I'm okay."

Right. So not okay. He had the lives of three people, four if you included Shadow, in his hands.

"Daniel, shine your light on the device."

His friend held the beam steady.

The darkness pressed in around him, and the smell of the damp earth and mildew tickled his nose. Odd. The odor grounded him to his task. He breathed in and out in a controlled fashion.

Using the stream of light, he traced the wires running along the door. He angled his light over the setup. A thin metallic strip above the latch confirmed his suspicions.

"Do *not* lean against this door. It's a magnetic switch." If the circuit broke, they'd all be nothing but a red mist.

"Can you disarm it?" Izzie's voice drifted from the enclosed room.

Logan glanced at the time and closed his eyes for a moment. "I think so."

"Not to pressure you or anything, but it better be more than a thought." Daniel's eyebrow rose.

Logan returned his attention to the device. Wires trailed down the doorframe to a crude battery pack wedged into the stone foundation.

He trained his flashlight on the battery pack. A single red wire fed into the detonator, and a blue wire ran back to the switch. If he cut the blue first, the switch might disconnect and trigger a detonation. If he cut the red, the device might have a failsafe and cause the C-4 to explode.

His mind bounced back and forth between the past and the present. Focus wasn't his friend. That had to stop. He drew in a lungful of air, retrieved his multipurpose knife from his pocket and opened the blade. The calming breath had little effect on this mental state, but as a SEAL he'd learned to push through even when he thought he couldn't. *The only easy day was yesterday.*

With shaking hands, he made the first slice. The plastic insulation of the red wire frayed. He peeled it back. Almost there. Logan held his breath. Dumb thing to do. So sue him. The woman he loved and his sister were on the other side of that door. He froze. Yeah, he loved Izzie. Always had.

He shook his head, dislodging the intruding thoughts, and made the first cut. The red wire snapped in two.

The silence in the cellar was deafening. Could Daniel hear his heart thundering against his breastbone?

"Well, are we going to blow to smithereens, or did you do it?"

Logan glanced at his friend. The man stood there with his palms up. He chuckled at Daniel's comical facial expression. That man and his sense of humor.

"One more wire."

"Then what are you waiting for?"

"For my pulse to stop racing." Logan rolled his eyes. The irony wasn't lost on him. He'd disarmed more explosive devices than he cared to count. None of them had his heart in his throat like this one. "Stand around the corner over there and take cover. Shadow, go with Daniel." Logan pointed, and Daniel and Shadow moved to the designated area. Not that it would do much good if the place blew, but it eased Logan's nerves. A bit. Maybe.

"Ladies," he called through the door, "go to the far side of the room and take cover if you can."

"Logan?"

"It's okay, Izzie. It's only a precaution." He hoped.

God, I could use a little of Your confidence right now.

"We've done the best we can," Izzie called out.

The trust in her voice was a balm to his shredded confidence. Logan wiped his sweaty palm on his jeans. Knife in hand, he snipped the blue wire. When the thing didn't explode, he closed his eyes and thanked God.

"Did ya get it?" Daniel peeked around the corner.

"Come on out, superhero." Logan's hands continued to tremble.

Daniel rushed over and worked the lock.

The door swung open. Logan brushed past Daniel and rushed inside.

Izzie peered up at him. When her eyes met his, she popped up and ran to him. Instead of throwing her arms around him, she cupped his cheeks. "That couldn't have been easy for you. Are you okay?"

He swallowed hard. Her concern for him fused his shattered pieces together. "I'm good." Logan returned her touch. "Izzie, I'm done worrying about how you'll respond. I love you and have since we were teens."

A smile spread across her face. "I love you too."

He pressed his lips to hers. All his fears and pain melted away with that single touch.

"It's about time." A soft voice had him pulling away.

Logan peered over Izzie's head. His twin sister's gaunt face stole his breath, but she'd never looked so good. "Lisa."

"Go to her," Izzie whispered.

He dropped his arms to his side. His eyes never left his twin. The strong woman he'd once known appeared broken and scared. The cement holding his feet broke apart, and he hurried to his sister. He tugged her into a hug. "I was so worried about you."

Sobs wracked her body.

Her thin frame registered. He pushed aside the emotions flooding his system. Easing his hold, he smoothed her hair. "Shh, it's okay now."

"Thank you."

"For what?"

"For getting us out of here."

"Speaking of..." He raised his voice so Izzie and Daniel could hear. "Let's get away from this room and that C-4. It's disarmed, but it still makes me itchy."

"An explosives expert who's worried doesn't fill me with warm fuzzies. Everyone out." Daniel shooed them toward the stairs.

"Bossy much?" Izzie shook her head and grimaced. With the little light available, Logan had tagged the bruises on her face and arms. Heath would become very familiar with the inside of a jail cell if he had anything to do with it. Izzie led the way from the dungeon-like room.

Lisa followed and took the steps at a snail's pace.

He and Daniel exchanged glances. A small breeze would topple his sister.

"Shadow, come."

The group made it up the stairs and outside.

Daniel rushed to Lisa, wrapped an arm around her waist and guided her to a pile of logs next to the cabin. She sat. Her shoulders slumped from relief.

Izzie spun in a slow circle. "Where's Heath?"

"We think he saw us coming and wasn't here when we arrived."

"We have to find him and stop him before he moves on and kills again." Izzie faced Logan. "Truck?"

"On the other side of the property along Mr. Gordon's fence line."

"Then let's go."

He gently clutched her arm. "Izzie."

"No. I refuse to let that man terrorize anyone else." She jutted her chin toward Lisa.

Logan's protective streak stood tall. "Let's get this guy. But first, you need shoes."

She glanced down and wiggled her toes. "Mine are inside the cabin, along with my clothes."

When she returned from changing, she was back in her own outfit and wearing her boots.

Izzie's hand brushed the length of his arm. With the sun illuminating her injuries, his determination to take down Heath grew.

Her hand slipped into his. "It's my job. Don't take that away from me."

"I would never do that to you." He squeezed her fingers. "Time for you to save the world."

She chuckled. "No. Just my little corner of it."

The idea of Izzie hunting down a serial killer twisted his stomach in knots, but he'd never treat her with anything but professional respect.

"Daniel, I might need Logan's SEAL skills. Stay with Lisa and call for help."

He shifted and peered into Izzie's green eyes. "Let's go get the bad guy."

She smiled.

"Shadow, come."

"Yo, Logan. You're going to need these."

He turned toward Daniel and caught the keys flying in his direction with his free hand. "Thanks, man." He pinned his friend with a stare. "I'm trusting you with my sister."

Daniel stared back. "And I'm trusting *you* with *mine*."

Logan nodded and tightened his grip on Izzie's fingers. "Ready?"

"More than." The bruises on her face gave him pause, but he refused to hold her back. She deserved to soar in life and in her job.

Trusting God to have their back, he sent up a prayer for safety and success. He jogged toward Daniel's truck with the woman he loved at his side.

FOURTEEN

Sweat trickled down Izzie's back as she hefted herself into her brother's truck. The height could have been Pikes Peak as much as her sore muscles protested. Her face hurt where Heath had used her as a punching bag in the name of discipline. The guy's twisted sense of marriage opened her eyes. In a way, her ex had wanted the same thing. He'd gone about it with mental manipulation where Heath had physically abused her into compliance all in the name of love.

She glanced at Logan, who slid behind the steering wheel. She paused clicking her seat belt into place. Logan had shown her love before he'd said the words. He respected her and her career. He hadn't bulldozed his way in and pointed out that everything she'd done was wrong. Not only that, but he'd taught her by example to go to God first instead of last. When he'd declared his love…it had been the proverbial icing on the cake.

His gaze drifted to her, and he froze. "What?"

Oh, nothing other than you're amazing. "You're kinda perfect."

He laughed. "I'm far from it." He turned the key, and the engine revved to life. "I meant what I said earlier."

"So did I. I'm just sorry it took me this long to admit it. I could have saved us both a lot of heartache."

"But we wouldn't be the people we are today without the pain."

She thought about it for a moment. "That may be true, but we lost ten years together."

"Then we'll have to make up for it." The truck bounced over ruts. His eyes flicked to her and back to the dirt path. He stopped at the county highway and handed her his phone. "Do what you need to do, Sheriff."

"Thanks." She grinned and dialed her office.

"Marshall County Sheriff's Department."

"Cory, it's Izzie."

"Oh, Sheriff, it's good to hear your voice. Are you okay?"

"A few scrapes and bruises, but other than that, I'm fine. Daniel is with Lisa Russell at a hunting cabin next to Gordon's property."

"You found her?" Cory's voice inched up an octave.

"Yes. The reception will be spotty out there. If Daniel hasn't already requested it, send medical, a deputy, and call in the crime scene unit."

The tapping of keys filled the otherwise silent connection. "Done. Now what?"

"I need all other deputies searching for Heath O'Brien. Stop him, but do not approach without backup."

"Heath's the killer?"

"Yes." The past eighteen hours had a lot of information to unpack. "Consider him armed and dangerous."

"You got it, Sheriff."

Izzie hung up.

"Where to?"

"Head to his house on the outskirts of town. He's on the run, but I'm guessing he's not expecting Lisa and me to survive, and he probably thinks everyone is focused on finding us."

"I'm sorry he hurt you." Logan's pained expression broke her heart.

Her fingers feathered the bruise on her cheek. "I'll admit,

it wasn't fun. But it could have been so much worse if you and Daniel hadn't found us."

"I should never have left you at the farm."

"Stop."

He jerked his gaze to her then back to the road.

"Do you trust me to do my job?" Deep down she knew he did. He'd proven it since he'd arrived in Rollins. But that didn't keep self-doubt from edging its way in.

"I'm a SEAL. I trust my team with my life. As far as I'm concerned, you and I are a team. You have skills. I believe in those abilities. I'd stand with you on any mission on Texas soil." He gave her a lopsided grin.

"Thank you." Izzie pondered his regret. "I know all about guilt. You've suffered enough from your self-imposed remorse."

"It's not that easy."

She laughed. "Easy? Who said anything about easy? You've shown me to put my faith in God. To turn to Him first, not as a later option. It sounds harsh, but you need to follow your own advice." And there it was again. Her directness. She shrugged her shoulders. She was who she was, and she'd no longer apologize or worry about her actions. Will's reign over her psyche had officially ended. Logan had given that to her.

His audible sigh filled the cab. "You have a point."

"Of course I do." She couldn't help flashing him a cheesy grin.

He chuckled and shook his head.

She filled her lungs with a cleansing breath. Their little conversation had allowed her to brush off the terror of being locked in a damp, dim cellar room rigged with explosives. Time to face the task in front of her. Finding and arresting Heath O'Brien.

Resting back, she rolled her head toward him. "We had it almost right."

"What's that?"

"The reason Heath abducted all those women."

"A strange fantasy of the perfect wife?"

"Yes, but not. He wanted to recreate his mother into the perfect wife and mom. And not the woman who left him in the hands of his abusive dad."

"Why now after all these years?"

"That's the question I want answered. If we don't get the truth from him, I'll dig until I discover what triggered him."

Logan glanced at her and smiled.

"What?"

"You. You're one determined sheriff. Most people wouldn't be concerned about the reason. They'd only care he's behind bars. You on the other hand scour for answers."

She stiffened. "And that's a problem?"

"Put your claws away. There's nothing wrong with it. I'm only pointing out that you're more detailed than most. It's what makes you great at your job."

"Oh." Yeah, she'd overreacted. "Sorry."

He raised a brow.

"Whatever." She gave a dismissive wave. One of these days, Will wouldn't live in her head. Then it dawned on her. Her ex wasn't renting space anymore, he only visited from time to time. Yup. Progress. She'd take it.

Izzie opened the center console, revealing a gun safe. She tapped in Daniel's code and retrieved her brother's backup weapon. She clicked in the magazine and secured the Smith & Wesson.

"You know how to speak my language."

Do what? She glanced at the gun. When his meaning hit her, she shook her head. Only someone in special forces would go there. "You're a dork, you know that?"

"Meh, maybe." Logan parked a block from Heath's house and cut the engine. Resting his arm on the steering wheel, he shifted to face her. "Izzie, I've said it a hundred times, and I'll say it a hundred more until it sinks in. You're amazing at your job. I've heard people talk, and I've seen it firsthand. Don't ever think you're less because of your brainless wonder of an ex."

Izzie giggled. Actually giggled like a teenager. "Will's a jerk. I already decided to banish him from my thoughts. But old habits die hard, so please be patient with me."

Logan reached across the seat and laced his fingers with hers. "As a SEAL, I've sat for days waiting and watching. I've learned patience to the nth degree. I think I can handle your ups and downs." He winked at her.

She pursed her lips to hide her smile. "Let's stop this guy, and then maybe we can focus on us."

"You've got it." He released her hand. "And you do know that I have your six, right?"

Izzie had lone-wolfed it for so long, the warmth flowing through her chest surprised her. "Back at ya."

They exited the truck, cut across the lawn of the adjacent house and edged along the trees lining the back of the properties.

She transferred her gun to her left hand and wiped her sweaty palm on her jeans before returning the weapon to her dominant hand. Forcing several deep breaths, her pulse slowed. Wow, time with Heath had affected her more than she cared to admit.

Logan's silent trek was impressive. The man moved like a shadow. She attempted to match his soundless footsteps but failed. Although, she'd done a pretty good job without his training.

The cell phone in her pocket buzzed. She retrieved it. Cory's name popped up on her caller ID. "Sheriff Sinclair." She kept her words low and quiet.

"Sheriff, Deputy McGregor called. Heath's at the rodeo grounds."

"Phil's keeping his distance until he has more backup, correct?"

"Yes, ma'am. He and Deputy Bennett have eyes on the suspect but are not approaching."

"Thanks, Cory. Logan and I are on the way." She tapped him on the shoulder and pointed toward the way they came.

He nodded and jogged in that direction.

She joined him. "Cory, did Daniel and Lisa's help arrive?"

Logan jerked his gaze at her.

Izzie listened as Cory filled her in. "Thanks. Let Phil and Jackie know we'll be there soon."

"Will do, Sheriff." Cory hung up.

"Well?"

"Paramedics are with Lisa now. They'll transport her to the hospital for evaluation, but from what I understand and witnessed, she's dehydrated and malnourished but has no serious injuries other than bruises."

Logan's steps faltered. He caught himself and continued his quick strides to the truck. "And O'Brien?"

"At the rodeo grounds. Phil told Cory he thinks Heath is gathering his things and plans to hightail it out of town."

"Then let's beat him to it." Logan sped up.

She met him step for step. "This has to end now." Izzie couldn't stomach another abduction and death of a woman to feed Heath's fantasy of the perfect life.

God, help me stop him. If at all possible, I want him behind bars. Not dead. But I'll leave it in Your hands how that happens.

Failure wasn't an option. The confidence she'd struggled to find flooded her. With God and Logan having her six, she wouldn't fail.

Logan's entire body sagged in relief at the news that Lisa's physical state wasn't significantly worse after being in the hands of a madman for two months. Her mental state? That was yet to be seen. It had killed Logan to leave his twin, but Izzie needed his military expertise. Heath had to be stopped. His skills would come in handy if things went south. He slid his gaze to Izzie then back to the road. He had full confidence in her. The mission would be successful one way or another. But his protective side insisted that he accompany her. With her cuts and bruises from her short time in captivity, along with the previous injuries, the woman wasn't working at full capacity. Still, she'd get the job done. And he would be there as her backup to make sure of it.

"What's the plan?" he asked. This was her show, and he refused to give her any reason to doubt herself again.

Smith & Wesson next to her, she gazed out the window. She stayed silent for so long, he thought she might not answer. "We'll join Phil and Jackie and get the lowdown. Then, I'll see if I can reason with Heath and get him to surrender." She shrugged. "If not, then I'll have to accept my actions and God's plans."

He sucked in an inaudible breath. She'd moved past going to God later and had given him control. "Sounds like a great idea."

She smirked.

"You're calling the shots." He winced. "Okay, bad choice of words. But this is your op. Tell me what you need, and I'll do it."

"It might come to taking Heath down if it means keeping the public safe and ending his reign of terror."

Yeah, he got that. He didn't fancy killing a man, but he understood the necessity if the need arose. "I'll do whatever it takes."

"Good. Because I'm deputizing you, effective immediately. That means you're acting under my authority as sheriff until we bring this guy in. You follow my lead and abide by the law—understood?"

He closed his eyes for a brief second. *God, please let this end peacefully.* "Understood." He knew she'd done it for his safety legally. But the weight of the implications sat heavy on his chest. Sure, he'd killed people during missions, but taking a life was never easy, even if it meant saving thousands of lives.

"I'm not trapping you, Logan. It's for your protection."

A laugh rumbled from his chest.

"What's so funny?"

"Nothing." He shook his head. "I'm used to being the one in protection mode. Not the other way around."

"Well, get used to it, buster. Unless we lied to each other back in that cellar, it'll be a constant between us."

"Yeah, about that..." The yearning to tell her he loved her again was superseded by the showdown they were heading toward. "I didn't lie."

Air whooshed from her lungs as if she expected him to say he was taking back his words. "Me either."

Funny how they both couldn't say the L-word at the moment, afraid that one wrong move could end everything.

Logan slowed the truck. He turned into the rodeo grounds parking lot and headed where Izzie pointed.

Phil and Jackie waved them over. Logan pulled to a stop and killed the engine.

Izzie slid from the passenger seat and clicked the door closed. By the time he got out, she was in a deep discussion with her deputies.

Logan and Shadow joined the group.

"By the way, I deputized Logan on the way here."

"Welcome aboard." Jackie shook his hand.

"Thanks. But I'm only here for one mission."

"Either way, you're a sight for sore eyes. Sheriff Sinclair is a fantastic boss, and we have a great department, but we're small. Extra help is appreciated."

Logan turned to Izzie. "What do you want me to do?"

"According to these two, O'Brien is in the horse barn. These two will monitor the outside, and you and I will approach with caution. I'm praying I can talk him down and arrest him. But if that doesn't work..." The words died on her lips.

He got it. He really did. He just hoped it didn't come to that. "Copy that. Loud and clear."

Izzie held her borrowed Smith & Wesson against her leg. “Let’s go.”

Logan released his SIG Sauer from the holster and mimicked her actions. They ducked and sprinted from one car to the next, taking cover behind each vehicle as they made their way to the barn on the other side of the grounds.

Izzie’s back pushed up against one side of the door, and Logan took position on the other. She peeked around the corner then pointed to the inside far corner with two fingers.

He nodded. The woman could be special forces with her professionalism and intensity. Logan smiled to himself. He’d love to see that. With her determination, she’d rock it.

She motioned for him to go high while she went low.

They advanced into the barn with precision. Their steps quiet and movements in sync with each other, not unlike him and his team.

He crouched behind a horse stall panel with a straight line of sight to where Heath hunched over and picked up a footlocker. Logan pulled in a deep breath. Izzie would put herself in danger in the next minute or so. He had to focus and not let his emotional entanglement with her affect his concentration. Another reason he shouldn’t consider working for her and should find a different job. One where he wouldn’t be responsible for her life. *Get out of your head, man.*

Izzie eased around the corner—weapon raised. “Police! Raise your hands where I can see them.”

O’Brien jerked his attention to Izzie and dropped the box. The contents spilled over the ground. He yanked a handgun from his waistband and aimed it at Izzie. “How?”

“That doesn’t matter.” Izzie’s shoulders tensed. Then, as if calmness washed over her, she stood straight with steady self-assurance. “You’re under arrest.”

The man shook his head. “I don’t think so.”

Izzie's tone softened. "Heath, those women were not your mother. I get it. I do."

"There's no way you can understand."

"That's where you're wrong. I judged relationships with all men based on my father's betrayal. And look where it got me. Alone and afraid of love."

Logan watched with amazement as she poured her heart out to the man who had hurt her and left her to die.

Heath stared at Izzie. "It's not the same. She left me with him. He became a drunk. Blamed me for her leaving and took that hatred out on me. Then I found her a few years ago. And you know what?" Heath's voice rose. "She has a family and is the perfect mother. Why couldn't she have loved me like that?"

"I can't answer that. But I'll let you in on a secret that I've told no one. Not even my family."

Heath cocked his head to the side, studying her. He was listening. And so was Logan.

"Several years back, I decided to find my dad. Give him a piece of my mind. I was angry and hurt, but nothing prepared me for what I found." She paused, releasing a long breath. "He remarried, and although he never had more children of his own, the woman he married had three. I watched from a distance. He treated those kids the way I dreamed of him with us. It hurt. But I started thinking about what I did have. I had my brothers and sister. My mom."

"I didn't have any of those things!" Spittle flew from his lips.

Izzie shook her head. Her relaxed demeanor shocked Logan.

"Maybe not. But you had a grandfather who loved you. I saw the picture he kept of you. You had friends who supported you. And you gave it all up. For what? A fantasy of the perfect life?"

Heath's gun lowered a few inches.

Logan eased his grip on his SIG and rolled his shoulder, never taking his eyes or his weapon off the man who remained a threat to the woman he loved.

A switch flipped, and Heath leveled the barrel of his gun at Izzie.

He lasered in on the man's trigger finger. One twitch and Logan wouldn't hesitate to take the kill shot if necessary.

"She should have taken me with her. I deserved the mother she became!"

Izzie appeared to clue in that Heath's thread of sanity had pulled tight, ready to snap. She took a small step to her right, leaving a bigger opening for Logan. Then another.

"I'm done!" Heath's finger wrapped the trigger.

Logan aimed and took the shot.

Heath's gun went off. The man spun and hit the ground.

Izzie dropped like a rock and didn't move.

He rushed over, keeping his aim steady and kicked the weapon away from O'Brien, who lay on the ground moaning. "Izzie?" No answer. "Izzie!"

"I'm good." She stumbled to her feet. Blood dripped from her arm.

"You were shot!" His heart pounded. He hadn't done enough. He'd waited too long.

"Relax. It only grazed me." Gun tucked into her holster, she clutched her forearm. "Is he secure?"

Logan nodded, unsure if he trusted his voice right now.

She retrieved the cell phone from her pocket and called her deputies who had taken up station outside the barn with an update. "You didn't take the kill shot."

Logan swallowed the emotion clogging his throat. "No. The man needs help, not death."

"I'd say you broke protocol and reprimand you, but I agree. Let's get him that help."

Phil and Jackie rushed in and took over the suspect.

Logan slipped his arm around Izzie's waist to steady her and leaned in. "You were amazing."

She chuckled. "If that were the case, I wouldn't be sporting a gash in my arm."

He shook his head. "Not true. It could have ended so much differently if you hadn't talked to him and shared your experience. Maybe that will go a long way in his recovery."

"If he *can* recover."

"We'll pray he does."

She smiled at him. "Let's take a look at the contents of his footlocker. It had to be important since he came back for it."

They strode to the mess on the ground. Logan's dog tags lay among other belongings most likely from the women Heath had killed. His trophies. Maybe the man was sicker than they thought, but he'd leave that up to God.

"Deputy Bennett, call medical for O'Brien then CSU to collect this as evidence." Izzie pointed to the mess. She glanced at her arm and sighed. "Not the way I wanted this to end. But I'm glad he's in custody."

"Same. Can we please get you to the hospital so the doctors can take care of that bullet graze and assess the rest of your injuries?" He placed his hands on her shoulders and gently turned her to face him. "If not for yourself, for me?"

"I'm not going to argue."

His eyebrows shot to his hairline.

She laughed. "Come on, Teamguy. Let's get me cleaned up and see your sister."

He snuck a kiss to her cheek and led her to the truck, thanking God the entire way for her safety.

FIFTEEN

One week later

The farmhouse on Stone Creek Ranch bustled with activity from the welcome home celebration for Cooper, Grace and Lexi's honeymoon slash family vacation, and Lisa's release from Heath O'Brien's clutches and her stay in the hospital. O'Brien had confessed to abducting and killing the barrel racers, and the grave at his grandfather's house had held Whitney Morris's body. The phone call to the young woman's parents and her boyfriend, Chase Fowler, had broken Izzie's heart. But at least they had closure. And as for Grey Chapman's disappearance, Kristi had called to tell her he'd taken a couple of days off and forgotten to put it on the calendar. Mystery solved there.

A few unanswered questions remained, but they'd have to wait. Izzie had requested two weeks off to recover from her injuries and spend time with Logan. One week into her leave, she sat on the couch snuggled into his side, watched the hubbub happening around her, and soaked up the love. The man had become her rock over the past few days. The nightmares had hit her hard. Every morning when they met in the kitchen for coffee to start the day, he'd hug her and encourage her to talk about her fears. They'd taken long walks on the ranch with Shadow pulling double duty for both of them. Her and Logan's connection had deepened through the shared experience. And she thanked God every day for sending Logan into her life again.

"Aunt Izzie!" Lexi skipped over.

"What's up, Lex?" Izzie's shoulder bounced at Logan's silent laughter.

"See what Momma got me while we were in Hawaii?" The young girl spun and tapped her head, showing off her new hair clip with hand-painted hibiscus flowers.

Izzie's heart burst at Lexi calling Grace Momma. "That's beautiful."

"Know what else?"

"What?" Logan asked.

"Momma and Daddy said I get a baby brother or sister as soon as they can make that happen." Lexi crinkled her nose then a huge smile emerged.

"Lexi Rose," Grace scolded. "That was supposed to be a secret."

Daniel waltzed in with a cup of lemonade in his hand and snorted. "As if. We all know you two plan to have more babies. Where's the secret in that?" Her brother did have a point.

Izzie couldn't contain her laughter any longer. "I'm excited for you, Lexi. You'll be the best big sister ever. Well, except for me that is." She grabbed Lexi, tugged her in and tickled her.

Lexi's squeals filled the room. "Aunt Izzie, stop."

She released her niece.

"Since the cat's out of the bag, let me know if you have any references for private investigators. I'll be adding a couple of employees to my business in the near future." Grace waggled her finger at Lexi. "You better watch out, little girl." With the fun-loving threat, her sister-in-law disappeared into the kitchen.

Lexi snickered at her mom's exit. "Gotta go. I promised to help Grandma." The bundle of eight-year-old energy flew from the room.

Logan leaned in and whispered, "I want ten of them."

"Babies?" Her voice squeaked.

"No. Goats. Yes, babies."

"Slow your roll, Mr. Navy SEAL. First of all, we aren't married. And second, if we're having ten, then you better figure out how you can have six to eight of them, because they aren't all coming from me." She narrowed her gaze at the smirk on his face. She elbowed him in the ribs.

"Ow, what was that for?"

"I saw that mischievous look."

He kissed her cheek as his twin sister ambled in and sank onto the recliner. Color had returned to Lisa's cheeks, and she walked without appearing like she'd fall over in a light Texas breeze. The woman was on the mend. However, the dark circles under her eyes told a different story.

"I never thought I'd see the day." Lisa pointed to her then Logan. "But I'm happy about it."

"Good." Logan playfully glared at his sister.

Lisa waved him off. "Thanks for letting me stay at the ranch."

"As if Mom or any of us would have let you be alone after what happened." Izzie glanced at Logan. When he nodded, she returned her attention to Lisa. "I want you to know, what happened was not your fault. You did nothing wrong."

Lisa's eyes widened, and her mouth dropped open.

"Don't look so surprised. Logan and I are the king and queen of guilt and self-blame." When Lisa didn't respond, Izzie continued. "PTSD is real. You don't have to be a soldier like your brother—"

"Sailor," Logan corrected.

She rolled her eyes, causing Lisa to chuckle. "Excuse me. A sailor like Logan, or in law enforcement like me. Anyone can experience trauma and the effects of it. The first step is to trust someone to share your fears with." Izzie rested her head on Logan's shoulder.

Lisa's forehead scrunched as if she was deep in thought.

Daniel shoved off the wall where he'd stationed himself as self-proclaimed guardian. "It's true, Lisa. Everything from car accidents to threats can trigger trauma." He motioned to us and toward the kitchen. "Most everyone in this house has experienced a life-changing trauma. And those who have, are all affected by PTSD to some degree."

Izzie jolted. Daniel. Her happy, class-clown brother had PTSD? She didn't think anyone in the family knew that. And what about Payton? Did he know something she didn't? She shook off the questions running through her mind. She'd dig into his statement later. "He's right, you know."

"Oh, please say that again." Daniel grinned like a fool.

Izzie shook her head. "You're a dork." She looked at Lisa. "See what I have to put up with?"

A genuine smile spread across her friend's face. "Brothers are pretty great."

Logan practically launched off the couch and gathered his twin in his arms. "Please don't ever scare me like that again." His muffled words brought tears to Izzie's eyes.

"Don't plan to." Lisa's watery response did it. Tears rolled down Izzie's cheeks.

Daniel patted Logan on the back. "I've got her. Why don't you go for a walk and burn off all that extra emotion."

Logan took a step back but didn't let go of Lisa's shoulders. "Are you going to be okay?"

A lopsided smile formed on his sister's lips. "You've been babysitting me on and off all week. Spend some time alone with Izzie."

Logan raised a questioning brow.

Lisa laughed. The sound was wonderful. "Go."

Daniel's gaze connected with Logan's, and he dipped his chin. What was up with those two?

Izzie rose from the couch and wrapped her arms around Lisa. "Don't let Daniel bother you."

"Hey!" Daniel held his hands out to his sides. "What did I do?"

"You're you. And we love you." She gave her brother a quick peck on the cheek then turned to Logan. "Ready when you are."

He laced his fingers with hers and tugged her toward the front door.

"Have fun kids," Daniel teased.

Logan glared at him.

Boys. Would those two ever grow up? She hoped not.

She squeezed Logan's hand. She had everything she wanted in life. A man who loved and respected her, a family she adored and a job she was passionate about. The only thing missing was the permanence of their relationship, but that would come. She hoped. For now, she'd bask in the warmth of having him by her side.

The birds chirped overhead, and the cattle bawled in the distance. Even the horses joined the symphony, easing the tension of the past couple weeks. He led Izzie to the far side of the barn toward a small fishing hole a little way away. Shadow frolicked in the pasture, having the time of his life.

When the last mission had devastated him, Logan never dreamed he'd find the peace that had blanketed him once Izzie and Lisa were safe. Izzie had been a big part of that. They'd shared their deepest secrets from the past, fears that continued to sneak in and take over, and the struggles from O'Brien's reign of terror. She completed him in ways he'd never imagined.

He wrapped his arm around her shoulders and tugged her close. She stumbled into him and laughed.

"Where are we going?" She rested her hand on his chest. "Because if you plan to walk to the next county over, I'm out." Her voice held a lightness he hadn't heard in quite a while.

He'd done that. Okay, so maybe he couldn't take all the credit. She'd started praying more frequently, so her relationship with God had a lot to do with it. But he secretly hoped he had a part in it.

"Just to the pond."

"And what? You're going to throw me in?" She snickered.

He halted, peered into her green eyes and studied her. "You really are happy, aren't you?"

"You have to ask?" She nudged him to continue walking, and he obliged. "The man I've loved since I was a teen is a real-life superhero, and he's here with little ol' me."

"Pfft. I'm not a hero. You on the other hand..." He kissed the top of her head. "You deserve a medal for not giving up on finding Lisa."

"Okay, so we have a mutual admiration society. Let's leave it at that."

Their boots crunched in the grass. The wildflowers were showing them the best Texas had to offer. He threw a quick thank you to God for the scenery. Logan wiped his sweaty palm on his jeans. Why in the world was he so nervous? It wasn't like he planned to ask her to marry him. At least not yet.

They approached the pond where they used to swim during the summer. He spotted the ever-present sitting log and steered her toward it. "Think you can handle sitting a spell with me?"

"Hmm. It'll be a hardship, but I think I can manage." She plopped down on the piece of wood and patted the place next to her.

Seemed Daniel had rubbed off on her. The woman was in rare form today. He shook his head and lowered himself beside her. He stretched his legs out front and crossed his ankles.

His brows drew together. What if? "Are you sure you're doing okay?"

Izzie sighed. She sounded content. "Logan, I'm dealing with the aftereffects of my abduction and the physical abuse. You know that. We've talked about it every day since it happened. Sure, it's always in the back of my mind, but I'm happy. Genuinely happy. My friend is safe, and you're here beside me. I have a renewed friendship with God. It's still difficult to think of Him in a fatherly sense, but I'm working on it. What more could I want?"

"I hope a lot more," he muttered.

"What was that?"

"Nothing."

Izzie picked up a rock and tried to skip it across the water. The thing sank like an elephant. She grabbed another and found a bit of success.

"You need practice."

She bumped her shoulder with his and laughed. "You're not wrong."

He inhaled, let it out slowly and shifted to face her. "Izzie, I didn't think I'd ever be whole again, but you gave this tired, broken SEAL hope."

"Back at ya, sailor."

A smile tugged at his lips. She remembered. "I've been thinking about where I want to go since my terminal leave will be up soon."

"And?" The worry in her eyes pinched his heart.

"I'm not sure what I'll do for a job yet. But I'd like to come back to Rollins. But I didn't want to presume you're good with that."

"Why wouldn't I be?"

"Because we haven't really talked about the future."

Izzie tilted her head. Her eyes stayed locked on his. "What specifically are you talking about?"

"Well, to start with, I want you to be my girl."

She lifted their joined hands. "And I'm not already?"

"I want to make it official." He cupped her cheeks. "Izzie, will you go steady with me?"

She blinked then threw her head back and laughed. The woman almost fell off the log they were sitting on.

Great. He'd made a fool of himself. He'd thought they had a connection. She'd said she loved him. Had even teased with him about babies.

Izzie's hand guided his face to look at her. "I'm not laughing because it's a crazy idea. I'm cracking up because I don't think that's what the kids call it anymore. You're showing your age."

His heart rate settled. "Well, what would *you* call it?"

"I have no idea. But how about this? I'm yours, and you're mine until the end of time."

"I like the sound of that." His lips twitched. "Izzie Sinclair, did you just propose to me?"

Her jaw dropped then laughter once again filled the air. When she collected herself, she snuggled into him. "I'm not ready for that, and I don't think you are either. So how about we agree to be in a committed relationship."

"That's perfect." He lifted her chin with his finger and lowered his lips an inch from hers. "I love you, Sheriff Sinclair."

"I love you too, Mr. Navy SEAL."

He erased the distance between them and kissed her, making it official. A promise of love, support and respect.

For now, dating the woman he'd dreamed about for years was enough. But later, he planned to make her his forever.

EPILOGUE

Fourth of July

The late-afternoon Texas sun baked everything it touched. Izzie couldn't be more grateful for the tank top and shorts she'd decided on for the family-and-friends Fourth of July celebration at Stone Creek Ranch. Logan, true to his word, had moved to Rollins. He'd accepted his twin's offer and moved into Lisa's second bedroom soon after he'd asked Izzie to be his girl. She smiled at the memory. Since then, they'd spent hours together, rekindling their friendship and more.

"What's that grin for?" Logan wrapped his arms around her and dipped down for a quick kiss.

"Oh, I don't know. Maybe I'm happy."

"I hope so."

"Yeah, some grumpy retired navy SEAL might have something to do with it."

A growl rumbled in his throat. "Grumpy?" He bear-hugged her and rocked back and forth, knocking her off-balance.

She tipped her head back and laughed. "You, you silly man, have changed my life."

"And you mine."

The scent of meat cooking on the grill mingled with the conversations and laughter of Izzie's family and friends, but she barely noticed as she gazed into Logan's eyes, seeing the love and respect she'd craved for so long.

"Aunt Izzie!" Lexi rushed over.

"What's up Lex?" She tore her gaze from Logan and focused on her niece.

"Daddy wants you."

"Oh, really?"

"Yes, hurry up." Lexi sprinted back to her dad.

"Apparently Cooper wants us over there." She pointed to the crowd of people gathering by the porch.

"Well, let's not keep the man waiting." Logan laced his fingers with hers, and they ambled toward the house. Shadow, who had been playing with the guests, trotted to his side.

Cooper stood on the top step with his arm around Grace. He cleared his throat, and the group got quiet. "Thank you all for coming today. It's nice to see the faces of friends among our family."

Izzie agreed. Family was amazing, but adding their friends made it even better. She rested her head on Logan's arm.

"First of all, food will be ready soon."

"Good, I'm starving!" Daniel patted his belly.

Cooper rolled his eyes. "You would be." A few chuckles filled the air. "After we eat, you're welcome to go to the barn and pet the horses or play the games Mom placed around the yard until it's time for the fireworks." A murmur rose for a moment then died down. "That's it for the schedule. But we have a couple more announcements. As you know, Grace and I took the long road to happiness." Cooper pulled his wife close and kissed her temple. "And life is about to become even better. Lexi, you want to do the honors?"

The eight-year-old hopped up the steps and spun to face everyone. "I'm going to be a big sister!"

A cheer went up throughout the crowd.

Tears pooled on Izzie's lashes. A honeymoon baby. Her

brother had been through so much. She was happy beyond words for him.

Cooper patted the air. "Thank you. Now for the next item on the agenda. Izzie and Logan, would you please come up here?"

She jerked her gaze to Logan. He shrugged and guided her to the makeshift stage.

"The mayor asked me to do the honors, and I'm thrilled to do it."

Izzie's forehead scrunched as she stared at her brother.

"Not long ago, Izzie and Logan teamed up together to find a serial killer. They not only found him but saved Lisa as well. We know you placed your lives on the line, and we are all grateful beyond words." Cooper picked up two blue boxes off the patio table. "The state of Texas and, more so, the town of Rollins is pleased to present both of you with the Sheriff's Medal of Honor."

Her mouth fell open, and her eyes met Logan's. He had the same reaction. "Cooper?"

Cooper opened one box, handed it to her, then opened the other and held it out for Logan.

"I don't know what to say." She swallowed the lump of emotion in her throat. "Thank you."

Logan glanced up at the crowd. "Yes. Thank you for the honor."

Cooper nudged Logan and lifted an eyebrow.

What was that all about?

Izzie traced the medal inside the box and smiled. Her ex Will's words no longer gripped her with doubt. She and Logan had taken down a serial killer. No one could deny her that accomplishment.

The chatter of the crowd in front of Logan faded into the background. He stared at the medal. As a SEAL, he never wanted recognition. But this. The acknowledgment was a balm to his soul.

"Logan?" Cooper whispered.

He blinked. "Yeah, sorry."

"You ready?"

A smile tugged on his lips. "More than."

Cooper chuckled. "Ladies and gentlemen, we have one more surprise for you."

Logan handed Cooper the medal box.

His friend took it and reached for Izzie's. The siblings played tug-of-war with hers, and the crowd laughed. Izzie let go and smacked her brother on the arm.

This was it. Logan had never been as sure of anything in his life. So why was he nervous?

He cleared his throat. "I'll admit, I'm a little stunned at the mayor's generosity including me in the medal presentation. It truly is an honor." He took a deep breath. "What many of you don't know…" He chuckled. "Or maybe you do. I fell in love with Izzie as a teen. But it took becoming a SEAL and a couple of tragedies to bring me to this point in time today."

He slipped his hand into his pocket and removed the ring box. He shifted to face Izzie. Going down on one knee, he gazed up at her. Her hand flew to her mouth. A collective gasp from below met his ears. He opened the box and held it up. "Izzie, you've been my one and only since high school. We might have lost our way to each other, but God orchestrated a reunion that neither of us expected. For which, I'm extremely grateful. I'm not a man of flowery words. So I'll get to the point. Izzie Sinclair, I love you. Will you marry me?"

Her head bounced up and down as tears spilled down her cheeks. "Yes."

He rose, slid the ring on her finger and kissed her in front of God and their family and friends.

"Okay folks, that's it for the show. Time to eat." Daniel shooed everyone to the buffet line.

Izzie's watery laugh made Logan smile.

"Was it okay that I asked in front of everyone?"

"It was beautiful. I loved sharing the moment."

"Good. Cooper told me it was a good idea."

"Cooper?" She scrunched her forehead.

"I know better than to ask permission from your brothers. You're a grown woman who takes down bad guys, but I did ask for his and Daniel's blessing."

She lifted on her tiptoes and kissed his cheek. "I love you."

He pulled her into a hug. "Good. Because you're stuck with me."

"Come on, lovebirds. Grab your food," Daniel called from a picnic table across the yard.

Logan shook his head. "Let's go before your brother comes and drags us over there."

"Have you decided about your job now that you're officially retired from the navy?" Izzie waggled her brows.

He laughed. "No. I'm not working for you. Although, I did consider it. We made a great team."

"That we did. But I understand. So what's it going to be?"

"Grace called a week ago. She offered me a job at her security company."

"But that's in Lackard." Izzie sighed. "I guess the commute wouldn't be too bad if we lived halfway between the two towns."

"No need for that. Living in Rollins was nonnegotiable. She agreed to allow me to stay here and work from home doing the research for investigations unless I'm needed on site."

"That was nice of her."

"I thought so." He leaned in and whispered, "I took the job yesterday."

Izzie spun and threw her arms around his neck. "I think you'll be amazing."

"I hope so."

"You will."

He kissed her. Nothing that lingered, but a quick I-love-you type. "One more thing."

"You mean the medal, the engagement and the new job announcements weren't enough?"

Logan laughed. "That may be so, but I have another surprise I think you'll like."

She sighed dramatically. "I can take it. Lay it on me."

"You're ridiculous."

"I know. Daniel taught me well. Now, quit stalling."

He couldn't contain his grin. "I bought a house."

"Seriously?" Her eyes widened. "When? Where?"

"Remember the Callahan farm? The one that his children couldn't sell for five years. The one you told me you loved."

"I remember."

"Well, the time condition expired. I bought the old place a week ago."

"You did?"

"Yup. I'm remodeling it and would like your input."

A smile spread across her face. "That homestead has potential. And it has a horse barn." She waggled her eyebrows.

He laughed. "I thought you'd like to have Firefly within stumbling distance."

"I've always loved that old place."

"That's good, since it's ours."

"Ours. I like the sound of that."

"Me too." He kissed her forehead. "Come on. Let's eat."

Hours later, Logan lay on the blanket Izzie had spread out on the grass for them to watch the fireworks. He stared at the stars dotting the night sky and thanked God for the woman lying a couple feet away. Shadow snuggled in on his other side and rested his snout on Logan's stomach. He threaded his fingers with Izzie's. "I couldn't ask for a more fitting end to our perfect day."

"Our own little family."

Contentment filled him. "When do you want to get married?"

"We've waited long enough. How about as soon as we can get a marriage license?"

"Three days for the waiting period. A couple days to finish plans. Next Saturday. Right here on Stone Creek Ranch."

She rolled her head, gazing into his eyes. "It's a date. I love you, Logan Russell."

Fireworks boomed in the background. The colorful display lit the night sky. But Logan couldn't pull his gaze from his fiancée. "And I love *you*, Isabelle Sinclair." He couldn't wait to make her his wife. He'd let her paint their house neon orange, as long as she was his forever.

* * * * *

If you enjoyed this Stone Creek Ranch book by Sami A. Abrams, be sure to pick up the previous book in the series

Christmas Rodeo Killer

Available now from Love Inspired Suspense!

Dear Reader,

Thank you for reading *Deadly Rodeo Threat*, book two in the Stone Creek Ranch miniseries. I hope you enjoyed getting to know Izzie and Logan. Painful pasts are hard to move on from, but with God and someone you trust by your side, anything is possible.

I'd like to send a shout-out to my awesome agent, Tamela Hancock Murray, and to my amazing editor, Shana Asaro. You two are the best! I absolutely love working with you. And thank you to my Suspense Squad girls. Knowing there's a group of writers who I can call at any time for writing help or just to laugh is amazing. Thank you, ladies. And to my writing community, you're wonderful.

Let's not forget a special thank-you to my law enforcement consultant, Detective James Williams, Sacramento Internet Crimes Against Children, who answers all my crazy questions. By the way, all mistakes are my own or are author privileges, so don't complain to him. Lol!

And thank you to my family for their love and support. Love you bunches, Darren, Matthew and Melissa!

I hope you enjoyed reading Izzie and Logan's story. If you'd like a BONUS SCENE, go to my website https://samiaabrams.com.

I'd love to hear from you. You can contact me through my website, where you can also sign up for my newsletter to receive exclusive subscriber news and giveaways.

Hugs,
Sami A. Abrams